THE AMISH CAT CAPER

ETTIE SMITH AMISH MYSTERIES BOOK 11

SAMANTHA PRICE

Copyright © 2017 by Samantha Price

All rights reserved.

No part of this book may be reproduced in any form or by any electronic or mechanical means, including information storage and retrieval systems, without written permission from the author, except for the use of brief quotations in a book review.

CHAPTER 1

As I stood at the front gate of the small house belonging to Ettie and Elsa-May, I hoped the people in the community were right that the two elderly ladies could help me with my problem. I hadn't seen them since I'd left the Amish community around forty years ago.

Looking down at Tom in his cat carrier, I could see he was anxious. His long, gray tabby fur was standing on end and his bright amber eyes were fixed on me, asking where we were. "It's all right, boy, we're visiting some friendly people and I'm sure they like cats. Everyone does." I closed the garden gate behind me and continued on the path that led to their front door.

I waited awhile after I knocked. I knew that, being in their eighties, the elderly sisters might take time to answer the door. When I heard the high-pitched yapping of a small dog, I held the cat carrier behind my back.

"It's all right, Tom. Mommy won't let the nasty dog get you. You're safe and sound in your basket."

Tom answered with a low growl. That was his, 'I don't like dogs, get me out of here,' growl.

The door was opened by Elsa-May holding a disagreeable-looking white dog in her arms. Elsa-May looked very different from how I remembered her. Now she was wearing glasses on the end of her nose, and her midsection had increased considerably. Of course, what I could see of her hair had grayed considerably, too.

"Molly Miller, is that you?"

"Yes. How are you, Elsa-May?" I nodded toward the cat carrier and held it slightly to one side. "And this is my Tom."

"Come inside and I'll put Snowy out the back."

I walked inside, glad that the dog was going out. Tom and I didn't like dogs; they had no manners and, if they weren't farm dogs, I didn't see they served any real purpose.

Ettie walked out of the kitchen wiping her hands on a tea towel. I sure hoped they wouldn't use that same tea towel to wipe the dishes later.

"Hello, Ettie. It's nice to see you again. You haven't changed a bit." I placed Tom's basket carefully on the floor, thinking how much older Ettie looked. She was stooped over, her hair was going white, and her face was more lined, but her beady eyes and tiny body were just the same.

"Molly Miller! I haven't seen you in many years."

She came closer and gave me a gentle hug while I patted her on her back as she did so.

Ettie's gaze dropped to Tom. "Who do we have here?"

"This is my best friend, Tom. We've been together awhile."

"Do you want to let him out?" Ettie asked.

At that moment, Elsa-May came through the back door and closed it behind her, clicking the dog door shut. "There. We're safe from Snowy for now. Would you like a cup of tea, Molly?"

"I would. Yes please. Shall I let Tom out now?"

"*Jah*, I'm interested to meet him," Ettie said.

"While you two are doing that, I'll make the tea." Elsa-May disappeared into the kitchen.

Poor Tom leaped out of the cat carrier, frightened to a frazzle, and I felt a pain shoot up to my shoulder as he stuck a claw into me. Then he proceeded to run around the sisters' living room before finding a hiding place under the couch.

"Molly, your thumb!"

I looked down to see blood dripping and I cupped my other hand underneath it. Ettie grabbed me by the arm and pulled me into the bathroom. She poured iodine on my thumb and wrapped it in a bandage.

"There now, all better. Does your cat usually attack you?"

"He was scared of the new environment, and he doesn't like dogs."

"Tea's ready," we both heard Elsa-May call from the kitchen.

"She has a loud voice," I commented quietly to Ettie who simply nodded.

"Come and sit down and tell us what you been doing these past years," Ettie said as I followed her into the living room.

Elsa-May sat there already, with tea and cookies on a low table in between the couch and a row of chairs.

"Where's Tom?" I asked.

Ettie said, "I can see his tail; he's still under the couch."

"Ah good." I sat down, looking forward to a cup of hot tea.

After Elsa-May had slurped her tea, she said, "Molly, I heard a whisper you're coming back to the community. Is that right?"

I was wearing a plain dress, but no *kapp*. I would soon have to wear one again. "Yes. And that has something to do with why I'm here today visiting both of you. People tell me if I have a problem, you'd help to fix it."

Ettie and Elsa-May glanced at one another, and Ettie said, "What kind of problem do you have?"

"It's to do with a man."

"We can't help you if you're looking for a man. We're not matchmakers," Elsa-May said sharply and to the point.

"Are you forgetting about Ava and Jeremiah?" Ettie asked her sister.

Elsa-May gave a low chuckle and then pushed her spectacles up onto the top of her head, pushing back her prayer *kapp*. "I'd forgotten about that. Well, maybe we can help you. Did you have a particular man in mind?"

"No, no. That's not why we're here."

Elsa-May leaned forward." Well, that's what you just said. Didn't you leave the community to become a teacher?"

"That's right."

"I would've thought schoolteachers would've been more accurate about what they say."

Ettie said, "Why don't we let Molly tell us why she's here? I mean why *they're* here?"

"*Denke*, Ettie."

Elsa-May reached forward and took a cookie, and as she munched on it, I began, "It's quite a long story."

"We've got all day long," Ettie said as she brought her teacup to her lips, her eyes fixed on mine. I knew I had to be accurate and precise around Elsa-May, and with Ettie staring at me waiting for a story, I knew it had to be good.

CHAPTER 2

I'D JUST FINISHED PUTTING the last decorating touches on my new home. It wasn't a new-build home, not even close to that, but it was new to me. I don't know what brought me back to live near my old Amish community that I'd left so long ago. I certainly don't have good memories of growing up with my strict, elderly *ant* once my parents died. But, here I am, and this is the place I've chosen to grow old in now that I've retired from teaching.

The stop at the small coffee shop had become a morning ritual on my way to the stores. Most mornings I went to the hardware store; there was always something that needed fixing or painting in the old renovator I'd bought. I took every opportunity to get out of my lonely *haus*. I'd come to realize that the hollow emptiness of my home was a reflection of the dark emptiness that lay in my heart. I tried my best to decorate my home to make it feel like a pleasant place. I filled it with flowers, fragrances and happy colors, but it still did nothing to stop the empty feeling in the pit of my stomach.

As I took my second swallow of coffee, my eyes were drawn to a man who had just walked through the door. I had no reason to notice him at all. He had his back to me while he gave his order at the counter and for some reason I could not take my eyes from him. He turned away from the counter and toward me, stuffing notes into his well-worn, brown leather wallet as he did so.

He looked up, presumably to find somewhere to sit. It was then that his blue eyes fastened onto me. I thought at first that he only looked at me because I was gawking at him. Normally, I would have quickly looked away if I caught a man's eye. Even at my age I was modest, as the Amish had taught me, but I ignored my inner promptings and continued to stare.

His features were not outstanding and he seemed as old as I. The lines in his weathered face had many stories to tell, I was sure. The wrinkles at the corners of his eyes deepened as his face crinkled into a smile, and he was still looking right back at me. I was surprised that a man could still make my heart beat that much faster. I knew him...yes, I knew him from somewhere, but where?

THE AMISH CAT CAPER

"Molly Miller?" My name rolled off his tongue like a well-formed musical note.

I looked at him a little harder, squinting to make my vision clearer since I'd left my glasses at home.

"Is that you, Jazeel?" Could it really be the first boy I had ever fallen in love with? Jazeel Graber from my old Amish community? I could not even begin to add the years; it was all so long ago.

"Well, I'll be. Is it really you? Is it really you, Molly?"

As he walked closer, I stood up. It seemed natural to hold each other even though I never embrace anyone and normally don't like to be touched. We clung to each other like two rats that were swept off a bridge in a rainstorm. He was the man I should've married. He had asked me when I was eighteen, but I'd had grander plans back then. Marriage and the drudgery of chores and running a household and doing what I was told...that, I'd thought, was not how I wanted to spend my days.

I left the Amish and followed my dream of getting my teaching qualifications. For years I'd taught other people's children. It was fulfilling enough, but what if I'd taken the other road? What would have happened if I'd married Jazeel all those years ago? I had come face-to-face with the man I'd left at the crossroads. Had I made the right choice all those years ago?

I wondered why I had turned his marriage proposal

down. In the moment we held each other, I ached for my lost *kinner* and *grosskinner* that I would have had if I'd said yes to Jazeel's offer to wed. Instead, all I had to show for my life that would soon be over, was an old wrinkly face, fading eyesight and an empty heart and home. Could it be that *Gott* was kind enough to bless me with Jazeel's embrace once more before my days on this earth came to an end? Even though my years of loneliness had steeled my tough heart, tears threatened to escape my eyes.

We shouldn't have regrets...or should we? What if we could have our lives over again, having the knowledge and wisdom that only age and many years of experience can bring? It seemed to me a cruel fact of life that youth is only for the young.

I did not want to be the first to pull away. I wanted to hold Jazeel forever. I closed my eyes and savored his touch. I would replay it all that night when I was alone in my small house. We pulled out of our embrace at exactly the same moment.

"Please sit, Jazeel, sit with me. Unless..." I looked around. "Unless you're here with someone else?"

"*Nee*, I've come alone."

Alone, but does he have a wife, a *fraa*, as the Amish would say? I studied his clothing and noticed that they were not Amish. He was clean-shaven with no hint of the traditional married man's beard.

Maybe he'd never married. No, he would not have stayed single, I told myself sharply. I didn't want to get my hopes up. I realized that even though I'm old and jaded, within me lay a spark of hope like a teenager would have.

Jazeel said, "I haven't been to a meeting for some time. I've decided to go back, though. I'm not in and not out. I guess I'm a bit of a backslider."

I giggled, like a girl. He had always been so funny. He sat down in front of me. His dark weathered skin had replaced the youthful honey-colored skin of yesteryears. His thick hair had thinned, and the color had faded, but inside he was the same man, the same Jazeel.

I wasn't ready to marry anyone when Jazeel had asked me all those years ago. I had been too young to know about true love and how rare it was. If I'd known then what I know now, I would have said yes. I had assumed in my youthful stupidity that when I was ready to marry, someone would appear. I did become ready some years later, but no man appeared.

Jazeel pulled his chair in toward the table, looked across at me and smiled. "Do you live 'round here now?"

"I've just moved back." I did not take my eyes from him. "And you?"

The beeper sounded, to let him know his coffee was waiting for him at the counter.

Ah, modern technology; apparently it was too much work for the waiter to bring the coffee a few steps to the table.

I kept my eyes on him as he walked to get his coffee.

His walk was slow and deliberate. He walked exactly the same way as when he was young, only slower.

Again, I savored every detail of his appearance, so I could think of him later when I was alone.

He returned with his coffee. Once he'd taken a careful sip, he said, "Tell me, did you end up becoming a teacher? I lost track of you."

"I did. I became a teacher, and did everything I ever wanted." *Except marry you*, is what I should have said. "And you? Did you get married and have lots of *kinner*?" The question was a tough one for me to ask, and no answer he'd give would make me happy. If he'd never gotten married I would be sad for him because he might have been as lonely as I. On the other hand, if he said he'd married, I would be unreasonably jealous. Jealousy is a horrid thing and no good ever comes from it.

With my hands under the table, I dug a fingernail into the palm of my hand to steel myself against his response. He had to have gotten married and had *bopplis*. The women had far outnumbered the young *menner* back then; that was one thing I clearly remembered.

He looked down into his coffee then set his eyes back on me. "I married. I married a *wunderbaar* woman. Jane, that was her name, and she went to be with the Lord two years ago."

I instinctively laid my hand on his. "Oh, Jazeel, I'm so sorry." I was ashamed of myself for hoping he wasn't married. I certainly was sad that his *fraa* was no longer with him.

He covered my hand as it rested lightly on his, blanketing it with the warmth of his other hand. "We had a *gut* life. Five *kinner* and three *grosskinner* so far, to show for it."

I wondered, is that how life is measured, by those we leave behind? If that's so, was my life all for naught since I leave no one behind?

"What are you thinking, Molly, with that faraway look in your eyes? You regretting turning me down all those years ago and running away from me?"

I studied his face; he was being humorous. I could tell by the twinkle in his eyes, even though his face remained deadpan. Did he guess I regretted my youthful ambitions? Most likely he did. He could always read me as easily as one would read a book: it appeared not too much had changed. I figured I should not play a game, as I would have done in my youth.

The young Molly would have replied, *Of course not, I've had a wunderbaar life.* As the old Molly, I said, "Yes, I regret not marrying you." There I'd said it. I not only said it to him, I admitted it to myself. I didn't know when I was young that I would grow old. Sure, I knew it: I knew that everyone gets old, but I didn't really believe it would happen to me.

He raised his eyebrows and shook his head at me. "You robbed me."

"Robbed you?" *Was he serious now?* I wondered.

"Robbed me of having a life with you," he said.

I withdrew my hand and leaned back as far as I could. I did not expect him to be so honest right back at me. For the first time, I realized that my bold and self-centered decision had affected someone I loved. It made me regret my decision that much more. It was a bold move in those days for an Amish woman to leave the community for a career. Careers don't last forever, but *familye* does. I could have put my effort into a *familye*, could have taught our own children. The career I'd left him and the community for was gone now, and I was left with only memories. If I'd married Jazeel, I would have had so much more.

I straightened my back and held my head up high. Regrets were useless and did nobody any good. What was done was done. Besides, I'd been a good teacher and I hoped I'd enriched my students lives, showing them love and kindness as I guided their young minds to appreciate learning and live a good life.

No words were necessary as Jazeel and I stared into each other's eyes, much as we'd done when we were teens. I knew that he still loved me; his gaze tugged at my very soul.

I took for granted the connection that we had. Surely only people truly in love can affect each other so.

He was the first to speak. "Where do we go from here?"

I laughed. *Where do we go from here?* Marriage was for the young. I was old and too independent now for my own good. Something had pulled me back here, though, to where I'd grown up. He was still looking at me; I had to say something. "Let's pick up where we left off." It could have been taken as a joke, but Jazeel did not laugh.

He leaned toward me. "I would like nothing more."

His blue eyes were drowning me; I couldn't breathe. "Oh, it's hot in here." I shed my jacket, draping it over the back of my chair. Was it too late for us? Could we take up where we had left off? It wouldn't be the same as it was before. It couldn't be the same as when we were young and carefree.

"I don't want to upset you, Molly."

I shook my head. "I'm not upset."

He took hold of my hand. "I want to see you again."

"You do?" That made me happy, but what if I got my hopes too high? What if we weren't as compatible now as we had been in our youth? Surely it was better to keep the memories pure rather than muddy them with a failed attempt at reconciliation. Or would we become two old fools in love?

Jazeel let go of my hand and laughed at me.

I waited for him to stop laughing. When he didn't, I said, "What's so funny?"

"You are."

I frowned at him, waiting for him to explain himself.

"You were so impulsive when you were younger and now you're scared to do anything; even something as simple as see me again. Are you scared you'll enjoy yourself?"

I snapped back, "I'm not scared." I wasn't scared to move back near the place in which I'd grown up. I wasn't scared to buy a house on my own and live on my own for all those years. "Are you trying to trick me into saying I'll see you again, to prove that I'm not scared?"

He nodded and chuckled again.

I'd missed his laughter. I figured we could be friends, if nothing else. He always brightened me up. "Yes, I'd like to see you again."

We talked a lot more while we sat in the coffee shop. We caught up on everyone we knew in the community. He told me about his *kinner* and what they were doing.

"Oh, Molly, I missed you so much."

I knew he meant it. I knew that he loved me dearly when we were young. It must have hurt him deeply when I left. I'd had to put all thoughts of him and the community out of my head and concentrate on my teaching. I told no one that I had grown up Amish for fear of being treated differently.

"So have you left the community?" I asked him about the community again, hoping this time he would give me more information.

"I haven't been to a gathering since Jane went home to *Gott*."

"I see." I went to take another sip of my coffee, but hesitated when I noticed it had grown cold.

Jazeel must have seen my hesitation. "Another coffee?"

I nodded. "Please."

As he rose to his feet and turned to order the coffee, I no longer felt alone. My bond with Jazeel had never been broken. I recalled that I had prayed to *Gott* to take my loneliness away. Was Jazeel an answer to my prayer? Maybe *Gott* was still watching over me. I sent a silent prayer of thanks, just in case.

Jazeel placed two cups of coffee on the table. I looked around to see that the surrounding tables were starting to fill, as it was nearly midday.

"Do you remember when we first met?" he asked.

I smiled. I remembered the first time I saw him. It was at his *mudder's* second wedding. Her first husband and Jazeel's *daed* had died, and it was her second marriage. Jazeel wore a black suit and he couldn't have been more than ten years old and I would have been eight.

"Let's not speak of the past today," I said. If we were to have some sort of relationship, I wanted it to be based in the present and not the past.

"You're as bossy as ever, Molly Miller."

I smiled while I slowly turned the spoon in my coffee, making a circular motion. "I suppose I am. Years of being a school teacher has probably made me even worse."

He chuckled, then rested his chin on his knuckles. "I want to show you my *haus*."

I pressed my lips together. I did not want to see his home where he'd had a life full of memories—memories without me.

As if reading my mind, he said, "It's a new place. I built it myself. I gave my old *haus* to my eldest son, John, and his *fraa,* Julie."

Again, he knew what I'd been thinking. "You built a house? I'd love to see it." The defenses I had tried to build against this man were wearing down.

I wondered; could our love exist outside the haven of this small coffee shop? I gazed into the distance and asked myself what I wanted to happen with Jazeel and me. *A life with him,* I told myself. I wanted to know love and the closeness of a husband before God took me home.

"Coffee gone cold again?"

I looked at him and then looked at my coffee. I couldn't have another. More than two cups in one day would be far too many, but I did not want this time with Jazeel to end.

"C'mon." He stood and held out his hand.

A light inside me beamed with happiness. I could only imagine the look of delight on my face as I put my hand in his.

"Let's get out of this place." He led me outside. "Where were you off to today?" he asked.

"I was going to the hardware store."

His eyes twinkled. "So was I."

I smiled as I looked up at his still-handsome face.

Nothing had changed. In my heart, I knew that *Gott,* after all this time, *was* still watching over me and wanted me to be happy.

Jazeel and I walked arm in arm, down the road and we're together until this day.

CHAPTER 3

"That's a lovely story, Molly," Ettie said, wiping a tear from her eye.

"And on a coming Sunday, Jazeel and I are rededicating our lives to *Gott*."

Molly and Ettie turned as one to look at Elsa-May when they heard a loud snore.

"I'm sorry about that, Molly. Elsa-May hasn't been sleeping well lately. It wasn't your story that put her to sleep."

Elsa-May slowly opened her eyes. "Did someone say my name?" She straightened her white prayer *kapp*, and then sneezed.

Ettie shook her head. "Never mind."

"And that's why Tom and I came to see you," Molly said to Ettie, ignoring Elsa-May.

"Why's that?" Ettie asked, frowning.

"As I just told you, Jazeel and I were going to start a

life together, and now he's gone missing. And I'm fearful something bad has happened to him."

"You and Jazeel? Who are going to start a life together?" Elsa-May asked. "I must've missed something good."

"I'll tell you about it later," Ettie said, a hint of annoyance in her voice.

"Jazeel Graber," Molly told Elsa-May.

Elsa-May raised her eyebrows on hearing the news, and then leaned forward and picked up her teacup. "We don't have to find a man for you?"

Ettie shook her head again at her sister. At least Elsa-May could've pretended she'd heard some of what Molly had said. *"Nee.* Molly told us that she met Jazeel again some weeks ago. He'd proposed to her when they were teens and Molly went teaching instead and left the community."

"What a lovely story," Elsa-May said with a smile.

"We both talked about it, Jazeel and I, and I was coming back to the community and he was going to start attending all the meetings again."

"You said he's missing?" Ettie asked.

"Jah, and I'm dreadfully worried."

"When did you see him last?" Elsa-May asked.

"At his house a few days ago. He was supposed to be coming to lunch in town with me yesterday, and he didn't meet me there. When he never showed, I went to his house and nobody was home."

"The logical thing to do is to ask Jazeel's *kinner* if they know where he is," Ettie said.

"I don't know where they are. Jazeel was going to introduce me to them soon. I only know a few people in the community. I suppose I'll get to meet everyone soon on a Sunday when I rededicate my life to *Gott*."

"Why don't you go home and not worry about anything. Ettie and I'll will find the phone numbers of Jazeel's sons and ask them where he is. We know where John and Jacob live, so if they don't have a phone in a shanty or their barns, we'll stop by their homes."

Molly nodded. "That would be good. *Denke*."

"More tea?" Elsa-May asked, looking down into her teacup. "This one has gone cold."

"Yes please," Molly said. "I'd love some more, too."

"And what about Tom? Would he like a saucer of milk?" Ettie asked.

"*Nee*, he's lactose intolerant. Many things disagree with him."

"Something must agree with him because he's quite a big cat." Ettie laughed.

"Tom's not overweight. It's just he's got a large frame and bushy fur. When I give him a bath you can see how slim he is. Tom only eats fresh meat, and he won't eat the cat food from the store."

Tom came out from under the couch and Molly leaned down to pick him up. He hissed and swiped at her before he ran away.

"Did he scratch you again?" Ettie asked, trying not to laugh at the cat's antics.

"It's nothing." Molly said looking down at her arm.

"Well, it looks like something to me," Elsa-May said. "The cat's wild."

"Nee, he's not! He's just a bit scared." Molly stood up and called to the cat. "Here, kitty kitty." When he ignored her, she sat back down. "I do hope Jazeel's okay."

"I'm sure there's nothing to worry about," Ettie said.

"We'll soon find out." Elsa-May said with a sharp nod of her head.

"Weren't you getting the tea, Elsa-May?"

"Jah, coming up." Elsa-May pushed herself to her feet and headed to the kitchen.

"We were going to have a future together, he and I."

"Has he met Tom yet?" Ettie asked.

As if hearing his name, the cat ran like a rocket into the kitchen and a squeal of fright was heard from Elsa-May. The cat ran from the kitchen just as fast, and headed back under the couch.

"I wonder where he's going. I should take him home." Molly stood up. "I might have to forget about that second cup, Elsa-May, but *denke,"* Molly called out loud enough to be heard in the kitchen.

Ettie stood as well. "Do you need some help to get Tom into the basket?" Ettie asked.

Tom ran back into the kitchen.

THE AMISH CAT CAPER

"I'll be fine." Molly picked up the cat-carrier and headed into the kitchen.

Once they were all in the same room, Elsa-May and Ettie looked on as Molly tried to coax Tom out from under the table.

Elsa-May pulled her mouth to one side. "Are you okay there, Molly?"

There was no answer just a loud crash as one of the chairs tipped over and the cat ran back into the living room followed closely by Molly. After which, Snowy barked and scratched at the back door.

Ettie and Elsa-May hurried back out to the living room to see Molly lying on her back. They both helped her to her feet.

"What happened?" Ettie asked.

"I overbalanced. Poor Tom, he's so frightened of your dog. Where's he gone?"

"Back under the couch. Is he wild or something?" Elsa-May asked.

"Nee. It's your barking dog that frightened him."

"Snowy didn't start—,"

Ettie dug Elsa-May in the ribs to keep her quiet.

"Why don't you open the basket and I'll get him in for you," Ettie suggested to Molly.

"Tom doesn't take well to strangers. If one of you can hold the basket open, I'll pop him in."

Molly carried the basket into the living room and Elsa-May and Ettie held it open while Molly somehow got the cat in.

25

"Now, how are you getting home?" Elsa-May asked.

"I sold my car and I go everywhere by taxi until I buy a buggy. Jazeel is helping me with that next week. Well, that is, if he ever comes back."

Ettie saw the look of utter hopelessness in Molly's face. "We'll find him. He can't have gone far."

"Leave it to us, Molly," Elsa-May said.

"Where are you living now?"

"I'll write down my address for you."

Ettie took down Molly's information in her address book.

"Denke. I noticed a shanty down the road not too far. I'll call a taxi from there."

"Do you want us to wait with you?"

"Nee, it's okay. Tom and I will keep each other company."

"Very good," Elsa-May said.

Molly, carrying Tom in the cat carrier, walked out the door and Ettie and Elsa-May stood at the front door and watched her go. When she got to the front gate she turned and waved.

"Say goodbye, Tom," Molly said to her cat.

Tom did not respond.

When Molly was out of sight, Elsa-May rushed to let Snowy in and Ettie collapsed onto the couch. Snowy ran around sniffing everywhere the cat had been, and Elsa-May sat down and picked up the knitting from her bag by her feet.

"That cat was wild and disagreeable," Elsa-May said

shaking her head. "I nearly opened the front door to set it free."

Ettie giggled. "Molly would never have forgiven you. She loves that cat for some reason. I can't see why. It doesn't seem to like her. Do you think the cat likes her?"

"Well, he tried to attack her every chance he got." As she knitted, Elsa-May said, "We should get going and do what we promised. We'll have to ask around and find the phone numbers for Jazeel's *kinner*."

"Just wait awhile to give the taxi enough time to arrive. We can't go down to the phone now. I've had enough of that cat for one day."

Elsa-May nodded and continued to knit.

"It's strange he would disappear without a word to Molly," Ettie said.

"Maybe Molly told Jazeel that the cat was part of the deal. Love me, love my cat. No wonder he disappeared." Elsa-May chortled.

"If Jazeel and Molly started a relationship like she thinks. then why wouldn't he tell her he was going somewhere? It just doesn't make sense."

"Do you think it's all in her head?"

"I suppose not." Ettie pushed herself to her feet. "The best thing I can do is find where I put my address book. I just had it."

"In the bureau drawer. Second one from the top. I saw you put it there."

Ettie scratched through the drawer. "Got it!" she

said holding it up. Once she flipped through it, she saw she had no phone numbers for John or his brother Jacob.

"We'll have to stop by John's house. He's closer than Jacob."

"*Jah*, we'll leave in half an hour, and then we'll go to see John first."

CHAPTER 4

*E*LSA-MAY AND ETTIE called for a taxi from the shanty down the road and then waited. When they waited, Ettie explained, "When you so rudely fell asleep on our guest, Molly was telling us how she suddenly met Jazeel again in a coffee shop while she was on her way to the hardware store."

"The last thing I remember her saying was some nonsense about his blue eyes and how it was all meant to be." Elsa-May shook her head making tsk-tsk sounds.

"I don't know how you could've fallen asleep. I found what she said interesting. I like stories about love and romance."

"Humph. I like more practical things."

"That was fast," Ettie said watching a taxi coming toward them.

They were surprised to see that it was Molly in the backseat. Then they realized it wasn't the taxi they'd called. She jumped out and ran to them as soon as the taxi stopped.

In one hand Molly was waving an envelope. "He sent me a letter. Telling me where he is."

"Where is he?" Ettie asked.

She looked down at the letter, and began, "Dear Molly—,"

"You don't have to read all of it," Elsa-May said, "just give us the condensed version."

Molly stared at Elsa-May. "I wasn't going to read it all to you, Elsa-May."

"Where is he?" Ettie asked again, aware that the taxi wasn't waiting for free.

"He's gone to look after his sick uncle."

"Has he given you a phone number of where he's staying?"

"Yes."

"Why don't you let the taxi go and you can call him and set your mind at rest."

Molly nodded and paid the driver and retrieved the cat carrier from the back seat.

"Oh, you've brought the cat again." Elsa-May screwed up her nose as she looked at the cat.

"Call him," Ettie urged, ignoring her sister's bad manners.

"That would be good. I just want to check that he's

all right." She called twice and each time hung on for a long time.

"Now I'm even more worried. Why is there no answer?"

"Did he say how far away his *onkel's haus* is, Molly?"

"I have an address. It's his *Onkel* Alfie."

"We know Alfie. At least, we knew him years ago. Elsa-May you remember Alfie Graber?"

"*Jah,* I do. I heard he moved to Reading."

Ettie turned to Molly. "Don't worry. I'm sure there's a reasonable explanation. He might be taking Alfie to the doctor, or something."

"Do you want to go there to check that he's okay?" Elsa-May asked. "Ettie will go with you."

"Would you do that, Ettie?" Molly asked.

"Um… sure. And Elsa-May would love to get better acquainted with Tom, while we're there. So leave Tom with her."

Elsa-May's jaw dropped open and Molly swung around. "Elsa-May you're so kind. Would you really do that?"

"Sure." When Molly looked at Tom by her feet, Elsa-May narrowed her eyes at Ettie and pressed her lips together so tight they formed a straight line.

"Tom likes to be around people," Molly said.

"We'd have to get a bus there. It's too far for a taxi. It'd cost a fortune."

"Why don't you both head off first thing tomorrow

then, and that way you can leave Tom at home, Molly," Elsa-May suggested.

Molly said, "It's a good idea to leave tomorrow, and in the meantime I'll keep calling Uncle Alfie's number, but, Elsa-May, will you still be able to babysit Tom for me tomorrow? He doesn't like to be left alone."

"The thing is that Snowy's an inside-dog. He goes outside to do his business and then comes back in. As we already know, Tom doesn't like dogs."

"Oh, Elsa-May, dogs shouldn't live inside. They belong outside; everyone knows that," Molly said. "Would you please babysit him, Elsa-May, just this once?"

"It won't hurt for one day, will it?" Ettie asked her sister.

Slowly Elsa-May nodded as her head dropped slightly and her lips downturned.

Ettie smiled. "Okay, that's settled. I'll find out the bus timetables and we'll leave first thing tomorrow."

"*Denke*. I knew you'd both be able to help me. I appreciate you looking after Tom, Elsa-May. It's a huge weight off my mind that he'll be in safe hands."

When Molly had called a taxi and left, Elsa-May and Ettie canceled their taxi and headed back up the road to their house.

"That was mean, Ettie."

Ettie didn't have to ask what she meant. "Well, do you want to swap and be there when Jazeel and Molly see each other and get all sloppy and romantic?"

"I see what you mean." Elsa-May sighed. "I suppose it would be easier to stay home with Tom. I just hope he doesn't take a swipe at me."

"Stay away from him. And we'll have to get fresh meat since he's allergic to everything else."

Elsa-May's eyes twinkled.

"Cut it out."

"What?"

"I know what you're thinking. Don't you dare give him anything he's allergic to."

"Okay."

"The cat might have some redeeming qualities once you get to know him."

Elsa-May chuckled. "As long as he stays away from me and my knitting that's probably all I can hope for. I don't know what I'll do with Snowy and Tom to keep them apart. You won't be staying the night will you?"

"*Nee.* We'll go up and back, and we'll be back by evening."

"I'll make a nice dinner and have it ready for you."

"*Denke,* Elsa-May."

"I'll have to keep Snowy outside, I suppose. I could put him in my bedroom for some of the time. He likes to sleep on the bed."

"Just make sure they don't get near each other or Tom will scratch Snowy to pieces."

. . .

Molly and Tom arrived at Elsa-May and Ettie's house the next morning. She'd been calling Uncle Alfie's number every couple of hours, but there was still no answer.

Ettie and Molly said goodbye to Tom and Elsa-May and then they headed to Reading.

From the bus stop, they got a taxi to Uncle Alfie's house.

Just as the taxi turned into his street, Ettie saw police cars and white vans. "Oh dear! That's never a good sign."

Molly looked at her. "What do you mean, Ettie?"

She nodded her head toward the police cars. "*That's* never a good sign," Ettie repeated.

The taxi stopped in front of the house. Ettie took a deep breath and looked up at the house, while Molly clutched onto her arm.

Ettie said, "Do you want to stay here and I'll go and see what this is all about?"

"No, I'll come with you."

As they approached the house, they were directed to stand back as the police stretched yellow crime scene tape around the perimeter of the house.

"What happened here?" Ettie asked one of the policemen.

"I'm afraid we can't release that at the moment."

"Has someone been hurt?" Molly asked.

"Yes, but we can't release any names at the moment."

Ettie said, "We know the two men who were supposed to be here."

"Mrs. Smith!"

Ettie knew that voice. She whipped her head toward the front door of the house and there he was. It was Detective Kelly.

CHAPTER 5

"WHAT ARE YOU DOING HERE, Mrs. Smith? Are you following me?" The detective looked at Ettie and then stared at Molly.

"No, I'm not."

Detective Kelly shook his head as he looked back at Ettie.

"This is my friend, Molly Miller, and we've come to see if Jazeel's okay because he came here to look after his Uncle Alfie and when no one answered the phone, we got worried."

"That's right," Molly added. "Is he here?"

He took the notepad and pen that he always had in a coat pocket. "Who was supposed to be here?"

Molly answered, "Jazeel Graber. He's a good friend of mine."

The detective looked far too interested as he scribbled Jazeel's name on his notepad.

Ettie added, "Uncle Alfie wasn't well and Jazeel came here to watch him for a few days."

"Well I've got bad news for you. The neighbor has identified the deceased as Alfred Graber. There's no sign of anyone else here."

"I'm sure you're mistaken, Detective," Molly said.

"I'll need to jot down some details about Jazeel Graber if you don't mind."

Molly proceeded to give the detective Jazeel's address.

"Isn't this out of your area, Detective? It's a long way from where you normally work."

"This is still in my jurisdiction for this type of crime."

"Crime? You think Uncle Alfie was murdered?" Molly asked.

"I don't think so, Mrs. Miller, I know so."

"Oh dear, that's not good. I think I need to sit down."

"Why don't you sit in my car for a moment and you can tell me more about Jazeel Graber."

Ettie and Molly followed the detective to his car and then got into the back seat. When the detective got into the front, he swivelled to face them.

"I'm assuming Jazeel Graber is Amish?"

"That's right," Ettie said.

"He was wavering in his faith since his wife died, but we were both going back on Sunday to rededicate our lives to God."

"Well, that's marvellous," Kelly said.

"Yes, it's a good thing. I left the community to become a teacher, you know."

Detective Kelly frowned. "The Amish have teachers, don't they?"

"I'm talking about a college-educated teacher at a school that goes beyond the eighth grade. I couldn't do that while living in the community."

"How well did you know Jazeel?" the detective asked.

"After I retired just recently, I bought a house back in my old community, the same community as Ettie and Elsa-May. The house needs many repairs and that has kept me occupied. I was doing the repairs myself. One day on the way to the hardware —"

When Ettie saw Detective Kelly's eyes glaze over, she knew she had to intervene. "I think all the detective needs to know is that you knew Jazeel as a teenager and you reconnected with him just recently, in the last few month. Isn't that right?"

"That's right, thank you, Ettie."

"And you've got no idea where he is?" the detective asked.

"As I said, he was supposed to be here looking after Uncle Alfie."

"Did you know Uncle Alfie?" Detective Kelly asked Molly.

"I remember him from years ago."

The detective looked at Ettie. "Did you know him?"

"Yes, but I haven't seen him in quite some time. Didn't the neighbors mention that Jazeel got here the day before yesterday? Um, today is Wednesday, so he most likely should've gotten here on Monday."

"I'll question them again. The neighbor grew concerned when he hadn't seen Alfred in some time."

"Oh dear, Jazeel's gone missing. I had a sinking feeling in my heart that something was wrong."

"Can we report him as a missing person?" Ettie asked the detective.

"He's certainly become a person of interest and we're as keen as you are to find him, Mrs. Miller."

"It's not Mrs. I never married. Jazeel asked me when I was younger and I said no and I never forgot him. And then I was involved in my career."

The detective gave a little grunt, and then said, "Will you ladies excuse me? I have a few calls to make." He stepped out of the car before they answered.

"Molly, do you realize that they think Jazeel might have had something to do with Alfie's murder?"

"Really? I never had any idea."

"Think hard, do you have any idea where else he could be, seeing as he isn't here?"

"No. He stated in his letter he was catching the bus to his uncle's house."

"Where is that letter?"

She tapped the bag she had brought with her. "I have it in here."

"Give it to me," Ettie ordered.

Molly opened the bag and handed the letter over. Ettie took hold of it and got out of the car.

"Where are you going with my letter?"

"Stay there." Ettie found the detective pacing up and down outside the house making phone calls. She waved the letter at him and he ended his call.

"What's that?"

"It's the letter Jazeel wrote to Molly. He tells her he's going to Uncle Alfie's house to look after him. Isn't that proof enough he didn't do it?"

"Mind if I hang onto this letter?"

"I suppose Molly won't mind, if it'll help you find Jazeel."

"Leave it with me. We're just as interested in finding Jazeel Graber as you are. I can assure you of that."

Ettie glanced over at her friend, hoping that the letter didn't implicate Jazeel further. "Can you tell me how Alfie died?" she asked the detective.

"He was stabbed."

Ettie gasped. "Who would do that to an old man who was not long for this world?"

"We'll do our best to find out. He put up a fight and as soon as the forensics finish their job, we'll do our best to establish if there's anything missing. The place was destroyed, like someone was looking for something. Now, if you'll excuse me, Mrs. Smith, I'll carry on with my job."

"Certainly, Detective."

Ettie headed back to Molly.

"Mrs. Smith?"

Ettie turned around when she heard Detective Kelly's voice. "Yes?"

"Would you like someone to drive you home?"

"That would be wonderful."

"If you can wait ten minutes, I've got a young officer heading back that way."

"Oh yes. We'll wait."

When Ettie got back to the police car she found Molly in tears.

"Oh, Ettie! It's just dreadful. I've waited so long to find the right man. I never thought I would, but then I did, and now where is he?"

At first Ettie had thought she was upset about Alfie, but then she realized Molly was upset about Jazeel being missing. "Don't worry. The detective said he'll find him. We'll go home and let them do their jobs. Detective Kelly has arranged for someone to drive us home."

∼

ALL THE WAY HOME, Ettie did her best to console Molly. It was only when they got back to Ettie's house and she was reunited with Tom that Molly calmed down.

Ettie opened her front door with Molly not far behind her. They closed the door quickly behind them so the cat wouldn't get out.

THE AMISH CAT CAPER

Then Ettie saw a peculiar sight. Elsa-May was sleeping on the couch with her mouth open, and the cat was curled up asleep at her feet.

Molly and Ettie silently laughed at the sight of them.

"They've become friends," Ettie whispered.

As they stared, Elsa-May slowly opened her eyes and moved her feet slightly causing Tom to wake. He hissed at Ettie and Molly.

"He's upset we woke him," Molly said. "He likes his sleep."

Elsa-May sat up and swung her legs over the side of the couch, careful not to upset Tom. "What happened?"

Ettie and Molly stared at each other and then they sat down and told Elsa-May about poor old Uncle Alfie.

"That's dreadful. Does Marlene know?"

Ettie had forgotten about Alfie's only daughter. "I don't know. I suppose she knows by now."

"If Jazeel wasn't there, where is he?" Molly asked.

"Detective Kelly's on the job. I'm sure he'll find him."

"Kelly's looking for him now?" Elsa-May asked.

"Ettie thinks the police now think that Jazeel had something to do with Uncle Alfie's murder. Oh, Ettie, is that our fault for telling the detective that Jazeel was supposed to be there?"

Shaking her head, Ettie said, "I don't think so."

"They'll find him, don't worry, Molly. And you'll be pleased to hear that Tom was well-behaved."

"*Jah*, he's always been a good boy."

"I'll put the evening meal on. All I have to do is heat it up. Would you like to stay, Molly?"

"*Denke*, but no. Tom and I should go home in case Jazeel comes back and looks for me there." Molly stood up.

"Shall we do the same thing as last time to get Tom in the basket?"

"*Jah, denke*," Molly said, heading over to the basket.

When Tom was in the basket, Elsa-May and Ettie stood at the door and waved Molly off.

Once they shut the door, Ettie said, "What do you think, Elsa-May?"

"What?"

"About Kelly thinking Jazeel killed Uncle Alfie?"

"If you two hadn't gone sticking your noses into things, Kelly would never have known he was meant to be there. Now it looks suspicious that he's not there."

"Oh dear." Ettie nibbled on a fingernail.

"We have to pray that Kelly finds the right person and that Jazeel is found."

"*Jah*, you're right, Elsa-May."

Elsa-May nodded. "As always. I'll heat the dinner."

"I'll let Snowy in."

CHAPTER 6

"*E*TTIE, it's Detective Kelly. He's just stopped his car outside," Elsa-May called out to her sister, who was in the kitchen washing the breakfast dishes.

"Good. Let him in."

"That's exactly what I was about to do."

It was the morning after Ettie and Molly had been at Alfie's house.

When Elsa-May opened the door, Ettie was right behind her.

"Detective Kelly, come in," Elsa-May said.

"Thank you. I have some news for you ladies."

"About Jazeel?" Ettie asked, following him through to the living room.

"Yes." He sat down on the couch and then Snowy woke, leaped out of his bed in the corner of the room, zipped across and started pawing at Kelly's leg.

Ettie said, "Elsa-May, put him outside."

"Stop that, Snowy. I'm sorry about that. He's taken a liking to you."

"Well, I'm not a lover of dogs." The detective stood up and Elsa-May swooped Snowy into her arms and took him outside. "I'll make you a cup of tea," Elsa-May said as she'd shut the door on Snowy and clipped the dog door shut.

"I don't have time for tea," the detective grumbled.

When both ladies were seated, Detective Kelly continued, "It looks like your friend, Jazeel Graber, is on the run."

Ettie raised her eyebrows. "What do you mean?"

"We found him in a jail up north. He's been arrested."

Ettie and Elsa-May stared at each other.

"Do you have the right Jazeel Graber?" Ettie asked.

"Yes, he's been accused of assaulting a bus driver at the Canadian border. He was taken into custody and the best we can surmise is he was trying to get into Canada with insufficient documentation. Looks like he was heading up there to make a new life for himself. He was pretending to be disoriented, but a medical examiner said there was nothing wrong with him. I had a talk with them and told them he was wanted back here on murder charges so they dropped the assault charges. One of my officers is heading up there to bring him back."

"Jazeel would never assault anyone. You've got the

wrong man," Ettie said. "Or else there's a lot more to the story."

He held his hands up. "Now before you say anything more, his prints were in our system and we found them all over Alfred Graber's house."

"How did his prints get in the system?" Elsa-May asked.

"From a traffic offense. You tell me he was Amish, yet two years ago he was driving a car."

"He left the Amish after his wife died."

"Well, he was kind of in and out," Elsa-May said. "Anyway, prints would be at the house because that was his uncle who died."

"Mrs. Lutz, he was making a run for it and that's something innocent people do not do."

Elsa-May leaned forward. "What kind of traffic offense?"

"Nothing too bad. I didn't take much notice."

"I know he didn't murder his uncle. You should know by now, Detective, that we aren't violent people."

The detective raised his eyebrows. "It seems nothing was missing in the house, so it wasn't a robbery. When we rule out robbery, it's likely the victim was killed by someone close and more often than not, the perpetrator is a family member," he said, "in roughly twenty five percent of murders "

"We'll have to find out who really did it," Ettie said.

"No! This is something you have to stay out of. I know you like to play detective, but it's far too dangerous. Someone has been murdered. Can I trust you to keep out of things?" The detective glared at Ettie.

"Yes, of course we will," Ettie said quietly.

"And what motive do you think Jazeel had for killing his uncle?" Elsa-May asked.

"They could've had a disagreement, or they could've secretly always hated one another. Things like that happening all the time in families. It's not unusual."

"Where is Jazeel now?"

"He's being brought back here."

"What did he say?" Elsa-May asked.

"He wasn't making much sense and that's all I know. So much for your friend's future with him. What was her name again? Molly?"

"That's right, Molly Miller. I'm sure there's some other explanation. You need to talk to Jazeel, or I should say *listen* to him, and find out what's really going on."

"We'll be talking to him, don't you worry about that!" The detective stood. "I'll leave you ladies to it, and I'll keep you up to date since Jazeel Graber is a friend of yours."

The ladies walked him to the door and when he'd driven off, Elsa-May closed the door.

"We'll have to tell Molly what we've found out."

"Elsa-May, we can't possibly. You saw what state she was in when she came home yesterday. We can't tell her that her beloved has been arrested for murder. No, we have to find out what's going on—and fast."

"But you told—,"

"Then I will be punished for telling a lie if *Gott* so chooses, but I will not stand by and let an innocent man go to jail. And, if Jazeel goes to jail that'll mean Molly will be spending more time over here because she doesn't know many people in the community. And do you know what that means?"

"What?" Elsa-May asked.

"Tom will be here more often too."

Elsa-May's eyes bugged out and her lower jaw fell. "That would be dreadful. Come to think of it, I should let Snowy back in."

Once Snowy was back inside, he sniffed everywhere Detective Kelly had been. Then he walked over and flopped down on his bed.

"What should we do, Ettie? Where shall we start?"

Ettie tapped a finger on her chin. "My best guess is to start with the neighbors. I say we go and ask them some questions."

"Why do you think they'll tell you something they haven't told the police?"

"It's been my experience that sometimes the police only hear what they want."

"Let's go."

"It's a long bus ride."

"I'll take my knitting."

"I'll pack some food for us to eat on the way," Ettie said.

Hours later, they arrived at Alfie's house and knocked on the door of the nearest neighbor. Since Alfie's house was on a corner, there was only one neighbor.

The place looked a little rough, the house with its pale blue paint peeling off and old rusted-out cars in the front yard. By the front door sat an old couch with holes in it.

Ettie knocked on the door.

"Hello?"

Elsa-May and Ettie turned, and saw a man walking toward them from the side of the house. He was a middle-aged man wearing gray shorts with a white singlet stretched over his stomach. He walked toward them, smoothing down his long scraggly hair.

"Hello," he said again, looking between the two of them.

Ettie introduced herself and Elsa-May, after which he told them his name was Dave.

"We'd like to ask you a couple of questions about Alfie, if we could."

Dave looked between the two of them. "Were you friends of his from when he was with the Amish?"

"We knew him, but we are mainly friends of his nephew, Jazeel."

"Do you know Jazeel?" Elsa-May asked.

"I do. I know him. He used to visit Alfie."

"If you know Jazeel, you'll know he didn't kill Alfie, but it seems the police think he did it," Ettie said.

"Do they?"

"Yes. And we're doing our best to find out what really happened, so Jazeel won't go to jail."

"Come inside. The front door's locked. I'll go 'round and unlock it for you. If you were friends of Alfie's and you're friends of his nephew, I've got a long story to tell you."

They waited at the front door and soon they heard a series of clicking sounds. Finally he opened the door. "Come in and take a seat."

Ettie and Elsa-May walked into the modest home and sat down on the brown couch as the man pulled up a chair and sat in front of them. The house smelled strongly of stale cigarette smoke and Ettie noticed two ashtrays full of cigarette butts on the windowsill. She hoped the smell wouldn't transfer to their clothing. Washing day wasn't until Friday, and Ettie was aware that she was wearing her last clean dress.

"I often looked out for Alfie. He wasn't too well these past weeks. I did a few things for him and kept an eye on the place, that kind of thing. I can't look after anyone too well, what with my own health problems. Someone needs to look after me."

Elsa-May leaned forward. "Tell us what you know. Who do you think did this to Alfie?"

"It's a long story."

"We're used to those," Ettie said.

"There's a man who used to own a car yard around these parts. His name's Joe Mulligan. Joe did some damage to Alfie's car a few months back. He knew it was his fault and he said he was going to pay for it. The damage was going to cost a fair bit. I think Joe knew some people –"

"You think Alfie was killed over a car, so the man wouldn't have to pay him back?" Elsa-May asked.

"I'm saying the man knew a lot of the wrong kind of people, and that's all I'm saying." He stood up and looked nervous. "That's all I should say."

"Didn't you say that it was a long story?" Ettie asked.

He shook his head and rubbed his stubbly chin in an agitated manner. "I don't want any trouble."

"We're just trying to clear Jazeel's name. How would that get you into trouble?"

"Forget I said anything."

Ettie and Elsa-May looked at each other and then stood up.

Just as they were nearly out the door, Elsa-May said, "Where would we be likely to find Joe Mulligan if we wanted to speak to him?"

"Down at Johnny's, the local bar. He's always there in the afternoon, from about four o'clock on. But don't tell him I said anything about him."

"Is he dangerous?" Ettie asked.

"No, I don't think so. No, he wouldn't be."

Ettie and Elsa-May walked out of his house. The

man walked outside with them. Ettie looked up and saw a woman walking up to Alfie's house. "Who's that, Dave?"

"That's Alfie's daughter, Marlene. I haven't seen her for years."

"We know her, Ettie," Elsa-May said.

"Yes, I know that, but she wouldn't remember us," Ettie said.

"Who's that with her?" Elsa-May asked, seeing a man who was wearing a dark suit and following behind Marlene.

"I've never seen him before," Dave said.

"Let's go over and find out, Ettie."

"Thanks for all your help, Dave."

"Dunno if I was much help."

When Dave walked back inside, Ettie and Elsa-May hurried over to say hello to Marlene.

When they went through the gate to Alfie's house, Ettie had a better look at the man's car and saw a real estate sign on its back window. "That man's a realtor."

"Are you sure, Ettie?"

Ettie pointed to his car. "It says it right there on his car. She's trying to sell the house already and Alfie isn't even in the ground."

"Where was she when her father was ill?"

"You knock on the door," Ettie said to Elsa-May.

"Why me?"

"You're the older sister."

"Okay. We'll have to find out what she's doing here."

Elsa-May knocked on the door. "Yoo hoo, Marlene. It's Ettie Smith and Elsa-May Lutz."

Ettie whispered, "She won't remember who we are. She would've been just ten years old when Alfie and his family left the community."

Elsa-May ignored her and walked into the house. "Marlene!"

Marlene came walking toward them looking none too happy. "Can I help you?"

"We're your father's friends. Don't you remember us from back when you were in the community?"

"I'm sorry, but I can't say that I do. I tried to put that whole episode out of my mind. You heard about my father, I suppose. Is that why you're here?"

"Yes, and we're dreadfully sorry for your loss," Elsa-May said.

"We never agreed on everything. Anyway, I suppose I've got the police to thank for this mess," she said looking around with hands on her hips. "I didn't realize it would be in such a bad state. Now I've got to employ cleaners to fix it quick before I put the house up for sale."

Ettie said, "Is that a realtor that came into the house with you just now?"

"Yes, the place is going on the market. Do you know anyone who wants to buy it?"

"No, sorry, we don't," Ettie said.

"If you'll excuse me, I've got things to do. Thanks for stopping by."

Elsa-May stepped forward. "Do you have any idea who could've done this to your father?"

"I've already been through all this with the police. I hadn't seen him in five years or more, so I was no help to them."

"Instead of looking for his murderer as if he had enemies or something, they need to be looking for the person who took my mother's diamond necklace. It was obviously a robbery."

"Was it worth a lot of money?"

"Yes, and my mother wanted me to have it. That was always the plan, but when she died my father refused to give it to me."

"Did that cause the falling out between you and him?"

"Let's just say it didn't help."

"What sort of necklace was it?"

"It was a single diamond. My mother won a competition. The prize was twenty thousand dollars, and she bought a single diamond with the money, and had it made into a necklet. My father was furious that she didn't do something he considered sensible with the money. He just wanted her to share it with him. He was mad. Mom just wanted something for herself because she'd never had anything nice."

The realtor walked into the same room and Marlene looked over her shoulder, and said to Ettie and Elsa-May, "Thanks for stopping by."

"It was nice to see you again, Marlene," Elsa-May said.

"And you. I'm sorry, I don't remember who you are."

"I'm Ettie and this is Elsa-May."

"Do you mind letting us know when the funeral will be?" Elsa-May asked.

"I'm not certain yet, but I'll let John Graber know and he can let all the rest of you know."

"Yes, there will be a few of us who would like to go to his funeral."

"Good." She pointed to the door.

When Ettie and Elsa-May were clear of the house, Ettie said, "Do you think the detective knows about the diamond?"

"Yes. She said she told him about it."

"When he was at our house, he didn't seem to think anything was missing. But then again, he wouldn't know if there was anything taken if he didn't know about the diamond's existence."

"She said she told him. Weren't you listening?"

"Nee."

"I know, you're thinking again, Ettie. You're thinking we should tell Kelly what Dave told us."

Ettie drew her lips together. "We told Kelly we'd stay out of things."

"You told him *you'd* stay out of things."

"He meant both of us."

"It's either that, or we go and talk to Joe Mulligan ourselves."

Ettie shook her head. "Kelly might run us out of the station."

"It won't be the first time." Elsa-May chuckled.

"Dave said Joe drinks at Johnny's every day. We could go there today rather than come back here another day."

"Ettie, we might not have to talk to Mr. Mulligan at all. And I'd rather not if he's dangerous. Why don't we tell Kelly?"

"Okay. I suppose you're right, but then he'll find out we've been back at Uncle Alfie's *haus*."

"It might be worth it if Joe Mulligan's guilty. Then he'll let Jazeel go, which will make Molly happy and Tom will visit us less."

"Good thinking, Elsa-May. Let's tell Kelly now."

CHAPTER 7

*E*TTIE AND ELSA-MAY were directed into Detective Kelly's office. He stood, and when they'd sat down in the chairs opposite his large desk, he sat down and asked, "What can I do for you ladies today?"

"It's about Alfred Graber," Ettie said.

"I figured as much. Do you have any information, or is it just a social visit because you think I have nothing better to do?"

Ettie ignored his comment, and said, "We went back to his house and Alfie's daughter was there. Did she tell you about the missing diamond?"

"Yes. I knew you two wouldn't stay out of it."

"I kept telling you she said she told him, Ettie."

Kelly said, "We've got it under control. There's no need to concern yourselves."

"She had a realtor there looking at the house to sell it," Elsa-May added.

He stared at them. "She didn't waste any time on that."

"That's what we thought. She wasn't very fond of her father, it seems."

"Would that be what the murderer was looking for—the diamond?" Ettie asked.

Kelly shook his head. "She put in a report with her father's home owner's insurance and if you ask me, she's gaming the system. I doubt the diamond ever existed. She can't show me any proof. And now you tell me she's selling the house as fast as she can; that tells me I'm right about the diamond never existing. Instead of asking about her father's killer, all she wanted to know was whether the police were finished inside the house so she could sell it. The woman's out for what she can get." The detective shrugged his shoulders and explained, "That's just what some people are like. Anyway, thanks for coming in, ladies, and giving me that information."

"What is happening with Jazeel?"

"We are expecting him back here late this afternoon. And then he'll go before a judge for bail tomorrow morning."

"Has Molly been in touch with you?"

"Your friend?"

Ettie nodded.

"No I haven't heard from her. For your sake, I hope he gets bail."

"So you still think Jazeel did it?" Elsa-May asked.

"In my experience when someone's murdered I'm firstly interested in the immediate family members, and Jazeel Graber was making a run for it. He had to be running for a reason."

"Before we go, Detective, the neighbor, Dave, also told us about a man called Joe Mulligan," Elsa-May said.

Kelly scratched the back of his neck. "Joe Mulligan—he's known to us. What did he say about Joe?"

Ettie and Elsa-May looked at one another.

Ettie said, "He owed Alfie money."

"Quite a bit of money," Elsa-May added. "And that's all we know."

Ettie pushed herself to her feet, and then the detective stood as well.

"Thank you for coming in, ladies. We're still investigating, so don't concern yourselves about that. Go home and bake cakes and knit socks or whatever it is you knit."

Ettie and Elsa-May walked down the steps of the police station.

"What do we do now?" Ettie asked.

"We should visit Molly and let her know that Jazeel will most likely get bail tomorrow morning. It'll be interesting to hear what Jazeel has to say."

"What about Jazeel's sons?"

"We can stop by John's place on the way to Molly's."

"Very good."

~

After they'd informed Jazeel's oldest son, John, that his father would most likely be appearing in court the following morning, they headed to Molly's house.

Just as they reached the front door, Elsa-May said, "It's getting late. We can't stay long."

"Okay we won't."

They knocked on the door and when it opened, Tom streaked through Elsa-May's legs like a bolt of lightning. Molly screamed and rushed past them and leaped down the five porch steps, beating the cat to the front gate where she caught him. As she held Tom in her arms, he squirmed and struggled.

"Come inside. I'll put him in the bedroom," Molly said.

Elsa-May and Ettie sat in the living room waiting for Molly to reappear. She came out a few minutes later.

"Do you have news of Jazeel?"

Ettie took a deep breath and told her everything they knew about Jazeel, Marlene, and Tom Mulligan. "We're going to check into everything, so don't worry."

"Will Jazeel get bail?"

"Probably. The detective didn't say he wouldn't get

it and I don't think they have any real evidence against him," Elsa-May said.

"Alfie must've been killed for the diamond since it was worth a lot of money," Molly said.

"The detective thinks the diamond never existed and the daughter is making a false insurance claim."

"I'm worried about Jazeel. I hope he's okay."

"We can come to court with you tomorrow morning if you'd like," Ettie said.

"Would you?"

"*Jah*, we will. And we've told John what's going on and he'll be there in the morning as well."

"*Denke*. John was the son he knew he could rely on."

CHAPTER 8

At court the next morning, Elsa-May and Ettie were sitting outside one of the courtrooms when they noticed Detective Kelly.

When he saw them, he walked over and crouched down in front of them. "I thought you'd be pleased to know that I talked with Joe Mulligan last night and he claims he didn't owe Alfie any money."

"We were told he damaged Alfie's car."

Kelly shook his head. "There was no police report made."

"That could be because Mulligan told Alfie he was paying it back."

"You're telling me this with second hand information—gossip, hearsay. You have no real facts. We have to deal in only the facts. I'm afraid we've come to a dead end as far as Mulligan is concerned."

"And what about the neighbor? He was the one who mentioned Joe Mulligan."

"I can't help that and I don't want to hear anything else unless they're facts."

"Excuse me, Detective Kelly," a uniformed officer said as he walked over to him.

Kelly looked at the officer and then looked back at Ettie and Elsa-May. "I'll talk to you ladies later."

∼

When I heard the judge grant Jazeel bail for fifty thousand dollars, I looked at John wondering how we could possibly raise that kind of money.

"Don't worry, Molly, they have bail bondsmen and I'll arrange it."

Jazeel turned and smiled warmly at me before they took him out of the room. I could tell that he'd missed me as much as I'd missed him. He was back home and he was safe. As soon as the police realized he wasn't guilty of anything, they'd drop the charges.

John and I stood up and headed outside the courtroom where Ettie and Elsa-May were waiting.

"He got bail," John told them. "I've just got to make some arrangements to get the money, and if all goes well he'll be out by the end of the day."

"Well, that is good news," Ettie said.

∼

It was three in the afternoon when Jazeel was released from the holding cell. He was so pleased to see John and me that he embraced us both.

"You don't know how good it is to see friendly faces. They think I killed Uncle Alfie."

"We know," John said. "I'll take you back to my *haus, Dat,* and you can rest there."

"There's nothing wrong with me. I'm just tired. I need to go home and sleep for a couple of days and then I'll feel better."

John ignored his father, and said to me, "You're welcome to come too, Molly, and stay for dinner and I'll take you home later."

"*Denke,* I'd like that. You should stay at John's at least for tonight," I said to Jazeel.

"Okay. I can see I'm outnumbered and I'm too weak to put up a fight."

As they walked outside, I asked, "How did you end up so far north when your letter told me you were going to *Onkel* Alfie's?"

"First, I got on the wrong bus, and then I fell asleep."

"How did you get on the wrong bus?" I asked.

"I left my glasses at home and I had a hard time reading the schedule. I told the police that and they didn't believe me."

I couldn't blame the police. It seemed odd. "How could you fall asleep for that long? The border's so far away."

"I had travel sickness pills and I had sleeping pills the doctor gave me, and I'd put both in the same bottle. I didn't want to take too much with me. I thought I'd remember which was which when I poured them into the one bottle. I've had trouble sleeping and I rarely take a sleeping pill because I don't normally like taking anything, even painkillers. Every time I've been at Uncle Alfie's place I found it hard to sleep, so I threw the bottle in with my things to take to his house." He shook his head. "I'd been asleep for twelve hours when I woke. I asked the man next to me where we were and then I realized what had happened. I went up front and talked to the driver and told him he had to stop and he wouldn't. He yelled at me to sit down or he'd call the police."

"What happened when you got off the bus?" I asked.

"Anger got the better of me and I got into an argument with the driver. And then the police were called. He raised his hand to me and I defended myself. The police asked to look at my documentation thinking I wanted to cross the border. Things went from bad to worse and I was arrested. They wouldn't allow me a phone call and didn't even listen to anything I said. I wanted to have someone else look in on Uncle Alfie and that's why I was so desperate to make a call. They threw me in a cell and the next thing I knew I was being brought back here for Uncle Alfie's murder."

From the front seat of the buggy, John said, "We'll work it all out, *Dat.*"

"I heard them talking about me, saying I murdered Alfie and that's why I was heading to Canada. I told them if I'd done that I'd be going south not north. And then I said if I was moving to Canada I would've taken more with me than just the clothes I was wearing and the small backpack. They didn't want to hear it." He looked at me and his blue eyes crinkled at the corners. "It sure is good to see you again, Molly. I hope they find who killed Uncle Alfie because I don't want to miss one more day of being with you."

I smiled at him and was pleased that he was making his intentions known in front of his son. He grabbed my hand and held it tight.

When we got to John and Julie's house, Jazeel headed to the shower while I helped Julie with the dinner, along with Julie's three teenage daughters. Seeing the three of them laughing as they scraped the peels from the vegetables made me realize again what I'd missed out on. My life had been lonely at the end of every day, once I'd come home from school. There was no one to share tales of my day with and no one to tell me about theirs. The girls were fascinated by my relationship with their grandfather and asked me questions in between giggles.

The girls fell silent when Jazeel walked into the kitchen. "That feels better," he said, looking all clean and fresh.

"Molly, why don't you and Jazeel sit in the living room and the girls will bring you some hot tea?"

"Good idea," Jazeel said before I had a chance to respond.

"I'll make the tea," the older daughter said.

"Denke." I walked out of the busy kitchen with Jazeel. I was so pleased to have him back, but fearful at the same time that I might lose my second opportunity with him. What if he was found guilty of Uncle Alfie's murder?

We sat on the couch together.

"Now tell me what's going on with you," he said.

"I've been so worried about you. I didn't get the letter until you missed lunch. It was the next day that I got it."

"Sorry, I found out that no one was looking after him when the housekeeper told me she was going away and she didn't think he should be alone. She cleans for him once a week and looks in on him from time to time. You don't have a phone, so I wrote to you."

I'd never had a landline phone after cell phones came into use, and now that I'd decided to go back to the Amish, I'd done away with the cell phone. The new house didn't even have a phone line installed.

Sally, the oldest daughter brought us out a teapot and two cups and saucers on a tray. "I'll bring back milk and sugar. I couldn't carry it all."

"Thanks, dear." When she walked away, I said, "I miss the energy of young people. That's what I liked most about teaching. It's nice to be around young people. They're so carefree and positive."

"I notice you talk about the past a lot. I hope you're not thinking about me and how I was in the past. I'm not the same man as the one you knew back then."

I stared at him. "No. I'm not. I know who you are deep down. People's true nature never changes."

"We must celebrate what we have today and not look behind at what has gone. Missed opportunities and missed chances are things to be learned from not things to be sorrowful over."

"You're right. See? You were always so sensible with your positive attitude, and you're still the same."

"*Jah*, I am. And I've been wanting to ask you something, Molly. Will you marry me if I don't go to jail?"

I smiled at him, having known that we were heading for marriage as soon as we both decided to come back to the community. "I will."

He picked up my hand and kissed it gently while his blue eyes never left mine.

A giggle escaped my lips and, feeling a little awkward under his gaze, I said, "I'll pour the tea."

"Have Elsa-May and Ettie been keeping an eye on you?"

"They've been helping me and now they're trying to find out who killed Uncle Alfie."

"That sounds dangerous."

"I don't know. They seem to know what they're

doing. I've heard they've done this kind of thing before."

When I handed him a cup of tea, he asked, "How's our Tom?"

"He's missing you and he's been rather grumpy."

Jazeel chuckled. "Tom's always grumpy."

"He had a hard life until I rescued him."

"I know." He sipped his tea.

"Would you be recovered enough to visit them tomorrow?"

"Ettie and Elsa-May?"

"*Jah.*"

"I'll be fine after I have a good rest. I can collect you mid-morning and we'll see them together."

"Oh, what about you getting a lawyer?"

"That can wait a day, or maybe two. I have some names from some friends I made in prison."

∼

AFTER I HAD dinner at John and Julie's house, they took me home while Jazeel went to bed. I hoped he'd be okay.

I walked in my front door and closed the door quickly behind me so Tom wouldn't escape. "Here, kitty kitty."

When there was no answer, I went from room to room looking for him and, eventually, I found him under my bed. "What are you doing under there, Tom? Come out now for Mommy."

Tom stared at me with luminous amber eyes. I reached out my hand to stroke him and he drew back and hissed showing his long white teeth and his pink tongue.

"What's wrong? Didn't you like your dinner? I know you don't like the dry cat food, but it is supposed to be good for you. It wouldn't hurt you to try some at least. Alright, Mommy will cut up some fresh meat for you, if you come out now."

I walked to the kitchen and pulled out the fresh meat. When he heard the knife on the chopping board, he was instantly sitting at my feet looking up.

"Who's a good cat?" I put all the chopped meat on the saucer and when I placed it next to him, he demolished the lot and I just got my hand away in time. "I'm going to bed now, Tom." I washed my hands in the bathroom and headed to the bedroom. I thought back to what Jazeel had said about living in the past, but that was my way of working things out. I'd felt lost for so many years and now I knew it was because God had not been the center of my life. It wasn't because I was without children or without a husband. I tried to fill the hole in the depths of my heart with my career, and it sort of worked for a while, but then my career came to an end and I was forced to retire. Jazeel was right about not looking back with regrets. The past was something that could never be relived.

I figured that the bishop would want us to wait a few months at least before we got married. I knew he would say that I should be settled in the community first before I married Jazeel. I was well prepared to wait however long the bishop thought I should.

I WOKE the next morning pleased to see the sunshine. I'd had a good sleep, although I remembered hearing rain at some point during the night, and I knew today was going to be a good day. Tom was even sleeping in the basket by the bed rather than under the bed where he usually slept. I sat up and Tom opened his eyes and looked at me

"Good morning to you, Tom."

Tom put his head back down on the edge of the basket.

After I showered, I put on the Amish clothing I'd been wearing since I came back and this time, I pinned my shoulder-length hair to my head and placed on the Amish prayer *kapp*. Never again would I have to bother with a flat iron. I made Tom and myself breakfast and then slowly did some chores until I heard Jazeel's buggy.

I laced up my boots and went out to meet him.

"*Guder mariye,*" His voice was bright and he didn't seem like a man who'd spent a couple of nights in prison.

"*Guder mariye,* Jazeel. Can you come in and help me get Tom into his cat carrier?"

"Where are we taking him?"

"To visit Elsa-May and Ettie."

"That's where we'd planned to go, but I believe they have a dog. Why don't we leave Tom here?"

"I could, but he was here by himself all day yesterday and I don't want him to feel like he's been abandoned."

Jazeel jumped down from his buggy. "Whatever makes you happy."

"We'll have to walk back into the house quickly, or he'll escape if we're too slow."

Jazeel and I managed to get Tom into the basket and then we headed off in the buggy.

I stared at Tom in his cat carrier on the backseat of the buggy. "Do you think he likes the buggy? He's only ever gone in a car before."

"He's not growling or hissing, so I'd say he likes the buggy very much." He chuckled.

"What's funny?"

"You are. What do you see in that cat?"

"He's a lovely boy."

"You're a kind woman. I hope you'll always treat me as well as you treat Tom."

I giggled and slapped him playfully on his arm. "You don't have to worry about that. We have a second chance with our love and we have to make the most of it."

"*Gott* has been good to both of us. That's why I know they'll find who did this to Uncle Alfie. They'll find out I had nothing to do with it."

"You should really wear your glasses more."

"I've got them with me." He patted the glasses holder on the seat between us.

I picked up the holder, pulled his glasses out and handed them to him. "If you couldn't see to get on the correct bus, you probably need them to drive the buggy."

He glanced over at me, took them with one hand while the other held the reins and put them on. Looking over at me, he asked, "How do I look?"

"As handsome as ever."

He laughed.

The buggy traveled at a steady pace down the winding roads toward the elderly sisters' house. We sat in silence—a silence where we enjoyed each other's company and neither one of us wanted to ruin our togetherness with unnecessary chatter. It was a perfect spring day with yellow wildflowers on the roadside swaying in the gentle morning breeze. Birds flew from tree to tree and chirped as they carried on their busy work of gathering twigs and dried grasses to build their nests.

It was always so fresh after the rain. The grass was greener and I could still smell the rain, which blended nicely with the freshly turned soil in the fields we passed. Jazeel successfully navigated the water-filled potholes, but we still had a few bumps along the way.

"It's so lovely after the rain," I said.

"I like the rain too. Not being in it. I like watching it fall and listening to it during the night."

"Me too."

"We have so much in common. We've got so much to talk about with our new life together, but first we'll speak to the bishop."

"*Jah,* that's best." I bit my lip, hoping that all would turn out well and they'd find Alfie's real killer. It was still hard to accept that something had happened to the poor old man. When we went through one of the many holes that the water had created, Tom gave a low growl of disapproval.

Jazeel said over his shoulder, "We'll be on a better road soon, Tom."

He spoke to Tom just like I did. Every day Jazeel was proving to be just the man Tom and I needed in our lives.

CHAPTER 9

*E*LSA-MAY AND ETTIE were finishing their breakfast when there was a knock on their door.

"Who could that be?" Elsa-May asked while Snowy yapped and turned about in a circle with excitement.

"Put Snowy out the back and I'll see who it is." Ettie stood up and poured the remainder of her hot tea down the sink.

When Ettie opened the door, she saw Molly and Jazeel, and then her gaze fell to the cat carrier in Jazeel's hands.

"Come in. You can let Tom out because Elsa-May's just put Snowy in the yard."

When all the doors were shut, Molly leaned down and opened the basket and Tom sat there. "He'll move when he's ready, I guess," Molly said.

"*Jah,* leave him be," Jazeel said, sitting down on one of the wooden chairs opposite the couch.

"I certainly had no intentions of trying to touch him," Ettie said. "Would either of you like tea or *kaffe?*"

"*Nee denke, Ettie.*"

The elderly sisters sat down with them and heard what had happened with Jazeel and why he wasn't at Uncle Alfie's house like he'd said he was going to be.

Ettie turned to Elsa-May, "See what happens when you don't wear your glasses?"

"Stop it, Ettie. My glasses are only for knitting and reading. I don't need them for anything else, like catching busses."

Ettie chuckled.

Tom suddenly leaped out of the basket and ran under the couch. Ettie lifted up her feet. "Will he bite me?"

"No. He only bites when you touch him," Molly said.

Elsa-May and Ettie exchanged glances.

"Molly tells me he's had a hard life," Jazeel said.

"Have I told you the story of how I found him?"

"No. Is it a long story?" Ettie asked remembering the last story she'd told them about reuniting with Jazeel at a coffee shop.

"*Nee.* It's short. I'll tell it fast. It was back when I had a car. I was driving home, just two streets from the apartment I had then, and I saw him jump out of a car window and the car kept going."

"Are you sure he wasn't pushed?" Elsa-May asked.

"I don't know, but I stopped the car and found him down an alleyway. He was all battered and bruised. I took him to the vet and they fixed him up. I tried very hard to find the owner—flyers, advertisements in the paper—and I couldn't find them anywhere. I gave up after a few months and now Tom and I are very well acquainted and I wouldn't know what to do without him."

"And what do you think of Tom, Jazeel?" Elsa-May asked.

"If he makes Molly happy, he's fine with me."

Good answer, Ettie thought. Good man.

Jazeel said, "I'm grateful to the both of you for helping Molly like you have."

"We didn't do much," Elsa-May said.

"Do you know anyone who'd want to harm Uncle Alfie?" Ettie asked.

"The only person I know is Bruno Gillespie, but last time I heard anything about him, he was in jail."

"Who's he?" Elsa-May asked.

"Bruno Gillespie committed quite a few crimes. He went to jail for breaking and entering but he could've gone to jail a lot longer if they could've proven what he had done."

"And what was that?"

"It must've been something pretty bad, like murder or armed robbery. Uncle Alfie would never tell me. But he told me that he had the proof right there in his house."

"Did Bruno Gillespie know he had proof?"

"I couldn't tell you that. That's all Uncle Alfie told me."

"How would he have come in contact with a criminal like that?"

"Uncle Alfie left the community years ago, as you know, and the area where he now lives is a neighborhood where criminals gather. There are always strange people coming and going at the house next door."

"Yes, we met Dave, the neighbor."

"Dave has always been good to Uncle Alfie. He's a good neighbor."

"I wonder if the police know about Bruno Gillespie. Did you tell them?"

"No, they weren't in the mood to listen to anything I had to say."

"You should tell them," Ettie said.

"They'll just think I'm saying that to get myself off the hook."

"We'll need to find out if Bruno Gillespie is still in prison or not."

"That could be why Alfie's house was in such a mess; because Bruno could've been looking for the evidence," Elsa-May said.

"I didn't even know my uncle's house was in a mess. No one's told me anything like that."

Molly put a hand on his shoulder. "I didn't want to

tell you anything that would upset you."

"We met Marlene at the house," Ettie said.

"She's back?" he asked.

"Apparently. She was there with the realtor to sell the house."

Jazeel shook his head. "Uncle Alfie hadn't seen her for years. They'd had a falling out. She's moving quickly to sell the place, isn't she?"

"She's the only child, so I guess there's nothing and no one to stop her," Elsa-May said.

"You really should tell the police about the man you just mentioned to us, Jazeel. They'd need to find out about him, and if he killed Alfie, you'd be free and clear."

"You're right. I will." He turned to Molly. "Will you come with me if I go to the police station now?"

"Of course I will."

He put out his hand and helped her to her feet.

"Oh, what will we do with Tom while we're at the station?"

"You could take him home on the way," Elsa-May suggested.

"Or, we could look after him," Ettie said smiling. "He's no trouble."

Denke, but I think it might be better if we take him back to Molly's *haus*. You've got the dog to contend with."

"Okay. Do you need help getting him into the basket?" Elsa-May asked.

"*Nee.* I'll get him if you can bring the basket here, Jazeel," Molly said.

Jazeel grabbed the basket and set it down in front of the couch while Ettie and Elsa-May stood well back. After the lid was open, Molly talked softly and kindly to Tom. He moved his head out. He looked at everyone suspiciously and then went back under the couch.

"Perhaps he'll come out for a piece of cooked chicken?" Elsa-May asked.

"*Jah,* he loves chicken. It doesn't agree with him, but a little bit wouldn't hurt."

Elsa-May went into the kitchen and came back with a thumb-sized piece of chicken and handed it to Molly who was down on all fours.

"*Denke,*" Molly said and then pushed the chicken toward Tom. "Here's some nice chicken, Tom."

Looking over Molly's shoulder, Jazeel said, "He's sniffing it. He's moving forward."

Then Tom's head appeared as Molly slowly pulled the chicken away from him. When half of his body was out, Molly let him have the chicken and grabbed him and popped him in the basket while Jazeel closed the lid and fastened it.

"Phew! I'm exhausted just watching that," Elsa-May said.

"He's shy," Molly explained.

When they were nearly at the front door ready to leave, Ettie asked, "Jazeel, before you go, do you know a man called Joe Mulligan?"

Jazeel scratched his head. "I can't say that I do. Why?"

"Nothing; it's just that Uncle Alfie's neighbor mentioned something about a man by that name. Forget it, it's probably nothing important."

The corners of Jazeel's mouth turned down. "If I hadn't gotten on the wrong bus, Uncle Alfie might still be alive today."

"Or you could both be murdered," Ettie pointed out.

"You can't worry about what might have been," Molly said. "You're always telling me that."

He slowly nodded. "You're right. I need to take my own advice."

"When you get to the police station, ask for Detective Kelly. He's the one in charge of the investigation."

"I've met him."

"Tell him everything you can think of, Jazeel," Elsa-May said.

He nodded. "I will. *Denke* once again."

When Elsa-May and Ettie closed the door on their visitors, Ettie headed for the couch while Elsa-May let Snowy back in.

Snowy scampered around for a quick sniffing session before heading to his dog bed in the corner, and Elsa-May sat down in her chair.

"What are we going to do? We know Jazeel didn't do it. We could find Joe Mulligan and talk to him. Kelly managed to find him."

"You're determined to talk to him, it seems. Uncle

Alfie's neighbor could've been making it all up about Mulligan and the man's already told Kelly he didn't owe Uncle Alfie any money."

"I can't just sit around doing nothing. Anyway, Mulligan wouldn't have told Kelly the truth. Didn't you hear what Kelly said? Kelly knows Joe Mulligan's name and that means he's been in trouble before."

Elsa-May folded her arms across her chest.

Ettie glanced at the clock on the mantle. "We could make it up there in time for his drinking session."

"Ettie, we're going to stand out like a sore thumb at the bar in these clothes."

"Of course, we are, but what can we do? Do you think we should disguise ourselves as *Englischers?*"

Elsa-May's jaw dropped. "Of course, not!"

Ettie chuckled. "There's not much we can do about it, then. We just have to go there and find the man and see what he's keeping from the detective. If Dave's right he's holding back a lot."

"Have you given two thoughts that this man might be the murderer?"

"And he might not be, but we're not going to get any closer to finding out who killed Uncle Alfie if we just sit on our backsides and do nothing. If he's the killer, he's not going to murder us in front of everyone in a public bar."

"I suppose you're right. And if we don't do anything, they might put Jazeel back in jail."

"Exactly."

CHAPTER 10

*E*ARLY THAT EVENING, two elderly Amish ladies walked into a bar and everyone turned and stared. Ettie and Elsa-May ignored everyone and walked up to the man behind the bar and ordered one soda and one iced tea.

"You ladies from around here?" the bartender asked once he'd delivered their drinks.

"No, we're not. We're looking for a man."

"Just one?" he asked, now resting his elbows on the bar, leaning over looking interested.

"One particular man. His name is... what was it again, Ettie?"

"His name is Joe Mulligan."

"Joe's here every day." He leaned even closer to them and pointed to a man sitting in a booth by himself with a beer in his hand. "That's him there. Does he owe you money?"

Ettie stared at Joe and then looked at the bartender. "No. He doesn't."

"Thank you," Elsa-May said to the man.

The bartender straightened up and grabbed a cloth and wiped the counter while Ettie and Elsa-May took hold of their drinks and headed to Mulligan.

"Mr. Mulligan?" Ettie asked.

He looked up. "Who's askin'?"

"I'm Ettie Smith and this is my sister, Elsa-May Lutz."

"What can I do for you?"

"Can we sit down a minute?" Elsa-May asked.

When he nodded, Ettie slipped behind the table and slid across leaving enough room for her sister.

"We're here to ask you about Alfie Graber."

"I thought as much when I saw you were Amish. Alfie said he used to belong to the Amish."

"That's right he did."

"What do you want with me?"

"We heard some talk that you might have owed Alfie money?"

"Have you come to collect?" he asked.

Ettie shook her head. "No."

"Not at all," Elsa-May said.

"We're not here about the money. All we're trying to do is find out who murdered him."

"It wasn't me if that's what you want to know."

"The police arrested one of our friends…"

"He was Alfie's nephew."

"Yes, and he was going to look after Alfie and then he got on the wrong bus."

"And after Alfie was found murdered, the police thought that our friend did it and we're trying to find some kind of proof he didn't do it, or find the killer."

"I hit Alfie's car. I rear-ended him. I knew I was in the wrong and I told him I'd get the money, but I didn't know how I was going to get it."

"Did you know Alfie before you crashed into his car?" Elsa-May asked.

"Yeah, we knew each other from when I had my car yard."

He tapped a cigarette out of his packet and offered one to Ettie and Elsa-May and they shook their heads. He placed the cigarette in his mouth and lit it.

After he inhaled and then blown a cloud of smoke up into the air, he said, "A couple of years ago I had to close the business like a lot of people had to do, so money has been tight since then. When I hit Alfie's car a few months back—his car wasn't insured and my car sure wasn't either 'cause I didn't have the money. I didn't know how I was gonna come up with that money. I was telling someone here one night about my problem trying to come up with the money—five grand —he told me he could have a way out for me. He told me he was a drug dealer and had to leave town quick."

Ettie and Elsa-May glanced at one another.

Joe continued, "Anyway, this guy said he had some cocaine left and I could sell it for five thousand and then he asked me how much I had. I only had six hundred and he said that'd be enough to buy it from him. We went out the back to his car, he opened his trunk and there was the cocaine. It seemed a small amount for that much money." He took another drag on his cigarette and exhaled the smoke slowly.

"What happened then?" Elsa-May asked.

"I had to find someone to buy it, didn't I? The next night when I was back here, I asked around and couldn't find any takers. There was a band here that night and two guys approached me and said they heard I had some stuff to sell. Then they told me they didn't have money and asked if I'd do a trade. They traded me an amp and a microphone. It looked pretty good quality and they told me I could get more than five thousand if I sold it. They were roadies. I figured I could put the things on Craigslist and I could get the money that way. I was nervous hanging onto the drugs and I was glad to see the back of the white powder. Then I took the amp and mike to Alfie's and asked him to hang onto them until I sold them. That way he'd see I was trying to get the money. Next night I see those two guys and they weren't happy. They dragged me outside into the alley and roughed me up."

Ettie gasped. "You mean it wasn't cocaine?"

"Or did they want more?" Elsa-May asked with eyes round like saucers.

"It was no good. I dunno anything about cocaine. I only smoked pot. It was white and the guy selling it looked like a drug dealer, so how was I to know? I'd heard that cocaine tastes sour on the tip of the tongue and this stuff did. I wasn't stupid. I tested it before I gave him the six hundred. These guys wanted their amp and mike back and I said I'd get it for them. They said they'd get it and made me give them the address and I said I'd have to go with them. After I gave them the address, they beat me up some more." He pointed to a faint bruise near his eye and a scrape down the side of his face.

"Do you think they killed Alfie?" Ettie asked.

"Maybe. They were angry."

"That was the night Alfie was killed?"

"Could've been."

"Why didn't you tell the police anything?"

"What? Tell them I sold drugs? They asked how I got the black eye and I told them I fell over walking home one night."

"What band were the roadies with?"

He nodded his head to a noticeboard near the door. "They'd be on that timetable up there. They were here last week and I don't know where they are now."

"Thank you, you've been very helpful."

"I hope they get 'em—the people who killed Alfie. He was a good friend."

Elsa-May and Ettie walked out of the bar and got a taxi back to the bus stop.

Soon they were heading back home.

"You were right to go, Ettie."

Ettie's face lit up. She wasn't used to getting compliments from her older sister. *"Denke,* Elsa-May."

"Maybe Alfie had hidden the mike and the amp and that's why the place was roughed up."

"That makes sense. We'll have to tell Detective Kelly."

"He's not going to believe second-hand information."

"He could come back and talk to Joe. I'm sure he'd talk to Kelly if he knew he wasn't going to be in trouble for anything."

"*Jah,* I think he would."

CHAPTER 11

THE NEXT DAY, Ettie and Elsa-May went to see Detective Kelly. Once they were sitting opposite him in his office, they relayed what Joe Mulligan had told them.

"So you want me to believe that Joe Mulligan sold bad drugs, and the people who bought them from him killed Alfred Graber? It was a drug deal gone wrong?" Kelly asked.

"Well, there's a few steps in between all that, but that's what we think."

Ettie pulled her mouth to one side. "What Elsa-May means is that we're not certain if we believe that, but it's a possibility."

Detective Kelly shook his head. "And then I have Jazeel Graber coming to me yesterday with a fantastical story about Bruno Gillespie." The detective made notes on the pad in front of him. "You said you had the name of the band the roadies came from?"

Ettie passed him the slip of paper with the band's name written on it.

"Can I keep this?" he asked.

"Yes."

A voice came from behind Ettie and Elsa-May. "Can I see you for a minute, sir?"

The sisters looked around to see an officer.

"Is it urgent?" Kelly snapped.

"Kind of."

Kelly pushed his chair out and stood up. "Excuse me, ladies."

When he came back into the room a few minutes later, he said, "I'm heading back to Alfred Graber's house. Would you like me to drive you back home on the way?"

"Yes thank you. That'll save us going by taxi."

"If you can wait here a few moments, I'll be back and then we can head off."

"Why's he going back there, Ettie?"

"He didn't say and with the mood he's in, I'm not game to ask him. The forensics have already done all they had to do. Maybe he's going to speak to Joe Mulligan again and he doesn't want to tell us."

Elsa-May grinned. "That's probably it. Or he could be going back to ask Dave if he saw people taking sound equipment out of Alfie's house."

"Are you ladies ready now?"

"Yes." Ettie and Elsa-May stood and followed the detective out of the building. They continued to follow him as he strode to his car, which was parked in the lot behind the station. He unlocked the door and opened it for them

"Thank you for driving us home."

"It's no problem I'm practically going right by your door."

Ettie frowned and was just about to ask why he was going back to Alfie's house when Kelly's phone sounded.

The detective clicked on the Bluetooth and answered the phone.

The ladies listened as the detective was told there was a fight going on between two women, and the address was Uncle Alfie's.

"I'll be right there." He glanced over at them in the back seat. "Would you ladies mind taking a detour with me?"

"We don't mind at all," Elsa-May said with a smile hinting around her lips.

"Did you hear the address?" Kelly asked glancing at them in the rearview mirror.

"Yes, Uncle Alfie's,"

"The plot thickens," he said.

"I wonder who the ladies could be."

"I wouldn't mind putting money on one of them being Alfred's daughter."

"Of course, that makes sense."

"I'll need both of you to keep out of trouble and stay put in the car when we get there."

"We'll keep right out of your way," Ettie said.

"The only way you can do that is to stay in the car."

Elsa-May said, "We will. Don't worry about us."

When they turned into the street, they saw two police cars. Kelly parked behind one of the police cars and Ellie saw Marlene surrounded by three police officers, and on the other side was a dark-haired middle-aged woman.

"Who could that be?" she whispered to Elsa-May while Detective Kelly got out of the car.

"I don't know."

"Let's get out and listen," Ettie said.

"Nee. Kelly has been good to us as so far, in giving us information. I don't want to upset him. He asked us to stay in the car and keep out of the way."

Ettie pushed her lips out. "I suppose you're right." She opened her car door hoping to overhear something.

Just as Kelly was about to get into the car, his cell phone beeped and he answered it walking away from the car. When Kelly got back in the car, he said, "It looks like we've found the diamond necklace."

"Alfie's diamond necklace?" Ettie asked.

"Yes, Alfred had a housekeeper. Some of my officers were called out this afternoon to a dispute, as you can see. The housekeeper turned up while Alfred's daughter was at the house. They got talking and the daughter asked her about the diamond and all mayhem broke lose when the housekeeper told her she has it. The housekeeper is claiming Alfred gave it to her."

"Oh dear," Ettie said.

"The other piece of information you might be interested in is that Bruno Gillespie got out of prison the day before Alfie was killed."

Ettie gasped.

"So you believe Jazeel now?" Elsa-May asked.

"It's given us something to look into, and we'll be following it up. Thank you for staying in the car. I thought you both might give me a hard time."

"You asked us to keep out of everything and we did," Elsa-May said.

"Good. Now I'll drive you home."

"Is it too much trouble to drive us to Molly's house instead? She doesn't live that far from us."

"Okay. Give me her address and I'll put it into the GPS."

After they were on their way, Kelly said, "I can tell you something, but I don't want you to get your hopes up."

"What's that?"

"Your friend might be in the clear if we can find footage that he was on a bus at the time of the murder. We'll be looking at the CCTV footage from the bus company to see if we can spot him."

"Oh good. When will you be doing that?"

"As soon as it arrives."

CHAPTER 12

When Detective Kelly approached Molly's house, Ettie and Elsa-May saw Jazeel's buggy.

Kelly's car zoomed away as soon as the sisters had gotten out, and they hurried to the door.

"I hope Tom doesn't attack us."

"He'll only do that if we try to touch him, Molly says."

"I certainly won't be touching him. You should've seen how deep the cut on her thumb was. And she's still wearing the bandage."

Jazeel opened the door before they knocked. "Hello. Molly is holding Tom while you get inside."

Elsa-May and Ettie hurried through the door to the sound of growling. They saw Molly crouching over Tom and holding him down. As soon as Jazeel closed the door, Molly let Tom go and he scurried away.

"Was that the detective?" Jazeel asked.

"*Jah*, Detective Kelly, and you'll never guess what happened."

"Sit down," Molly said.

When they were seated, Ettie told them about the housekeeper and the diamond.

"That's right. Uncle Alfie gave the necklace to Dawn because she's always been so good to him. She was always taking him hot meals and cleaning his house. He paid her for cleaning once a week, and she regularly did far more than what he paid her for."

"Do you know if there's any proof Alfie gave her the necklace?"

"I was there when he gave it to her."

"Oh, Marlene's not going to like that," Ettie said.

"Dawn was reluctant to take it, but Alfie insisted, saying his daughter didn't give two hoots about him. I don't remember if I told you this or not, but it was Dawn who called me and asked me to stay with Alfie for a few days. She was due to go on vacation with her family and she told me he'd developed a nasty cough."

"That's interesting," Elsa-May said.

"Marlene's claiming that Dawn stole the diamond."

Jazeel shook his head. "Where was Marlene when her father needed her? I do know that he hadn't seen her for at least five years. That's what he told me."

"Kelly was wrong about Marlene falsifying an insurance claim, anyway, because the diamond existed after all."

"We found out something else from the detective, Jazeel."

"That's right. We found out that Bruno Gillespie was released from prison last week. Before Alfie was killed."

"Have they questioned him yet?"

"We don't know about that. I don't think so, but they will."

"The funeral is on Monday. John was over here earlier and said that Marlene called and told him this morning."

"Where is it being held?"

"John asked if he could have the viewing at his house and give him an Amish funeral, but she refused and said she's having a service at the graveyard with a non-denominational minister leading the service. John asked if the bishop could say a few words but she flatly refused."

"Ah, that's a pity," Elsa-May said.

"I'll give you the address before you leave," Molly said.

Denke," Ettie said while trying to keep her eye on Tom, who was now sitting on top of his closed cat carrier.

Elsa-May turned to Jazeel. "Have you given some thought to what information Alfie had about Bruno?"

"I've been thinking hard. I asked him once but he didn't tell me. All I can remember was it was some crime the man had done and Alfie was keeping the evidence at the house."

"And the man knew Uncle Alfie had the evidence?" Elsa-May asked.

"I'm not sure, but I think so."

"Just as well you don't know," said Molly, "or you might have ended up the same way as Uncle Alfie."

Ettie sighed. "Why would your uncle keep evidence about a crime?"

Molly said, "Perhaps he was scared of him or what he would do."

It seemed to Ettie that if it were true, there was something more to it. Things just didn't add up.

CHAPTER 13

MAUREEN AND HER HUSBAND, Max, were the only *Englischers* that Ettie could see at Uncle Alfie's funeral.

Ettie and Elsa-May had gotten out of the taxi at the chapel in the grounds of the *Englisch* cemetery and joined the crowd waiting to go inside. As they waited, they were soon joined by Jazeel and Molly.

"Dawn Wilson is here," Jazeel whispered.

"The housekeeper?" Ettie asked.

"Jah."

"I hope she's not wearing the diamond."

"It looks like we might be in for a fun funeral with Dawn and Marlene together. I hope they've managed to sort out the thing about the diamond," Elsa-May said.

"I haven't heard anything about it," Jazeel said.

"Maybe they could cut it in half. That's what King

Solomon would've suggested." Ettie giggled at her own words.

"Ettie, don't mention the diamond today. It's not the time or the place."

"Technically, we're not at the funeral until we get inside the chapel. Anyway, of course, I won't mention it."

"Why haven't they opened the doors yet?" Jazeel asked.

Just then the double doors of the chapel were opened from the inside and a man with black robes and a white collar welcomed everyone in.

"This is dreadful," Ettie said. "Alfie would've wanted an Amish funeral."

"There's nothing we can do about that now, Ettie. Marlene was his only child and she has all the say."

Ettie screwed up her nose. When everyone started moving in, Ettie told her sister and Molly and Jazeel, "You three go ahead. I'll join you in a minute."

"What's wrong?" Elsa-May asked. "Do you need a tissue?"

"Nee. I'm okay. I just need a moment."

"Suit yourself." Elsa-May walked into the chapel with Jazeel and Molly.

When everyone else was inside, Ettie was just about to go in too when she saw Detective Kelly walking toward the chapel, so she waited for him.

"It's nice of you to come"

THE AMISH CAT CAPER

"I didn't know him, but I wanted to pay my respects. No one deserves to die in that way."

Ettie nodded, and wanted to believe he was there out of respect, but he'd told her many times that he always attended the funerals of murder victims to see who showed up.

They both walked in and found that the chapel was nearly full, so they had to sit in the back row. The rows had seats that had to be pulled down to sit on, although the backs were fixed. Ettie looked down at her black lace-up shoes against the deep red carpet. *Scarlet,* she thought. *That's what I'd call that color.* The carpet also had a fine black swirled pattern in it. She thought it was too fussy-looking. When Ettie looked toward the front, she saw the minister standing beside a wooden coffin that was flanked by two large bowls of white flowers. On a stage behind the minister was a large organ with pipes rising all the way to the large vaulted ceiling.

The minister opened in prayer and then said a few words about Alfie, which made Ettie cross because she could tell that the minister had never met him. The organ sounded and everyone stood to sing a hymn, accompanied by the loud music.

The closed casket was at the front of the chapel and Ettie couldn't help but wonder what Alfie would make of it all if he were looking on. The Amish never sang to a musical accompaniment in their meetings or at their funerals. Ettie was pleased to know that she had no intention of dying outside the community, and her children would know better than to give her anything other than an Amish funeral.

When the singing was over, Marlene read Psalm twenty three. After that, she sat back down and the minister introduced another hymn. A final prayer was said and then it was over. The minister then invited everyone to have refreshments in a dining room next to the chapel.

"Is that it?" Ettie whispered to the detective.

"I've been here for funerals before. They bury the coffin in the grave and no one gathers around to watch, not like they do at other places, or at your funerals."

"I see." When Ettie saw everyone leaving, she said, "I should join the others, and I'll let you do what you came here to do."

"Yes, I'll pay my respects to Alfred's daughter and her husband."

Ettie found Elsa-May in the dining room reaching for a cupcake.

"What did you think of the funeral?" Ettie asked her sister.

"It was about what I expected—nothing more and nothing less." Her eyes sparkled as she looked back on the cupcakes. "These cakes look good."

"Elsa-May, don't you think it's dreadful? Alfie wouldn't have wanted a funeral like that."

Elsa-May had just taken a big bite from a pink

cupcake with blue frosting. When she swallowed, she said, "Why worry? It won't affect where he'll end up."

Ettie frowned. "I suppose you're right."

"Of course I'm right. Another thing I'm right about are these cupcakes being scrumptious. Have one."

Sweeping her eyes across the array of cakes and small triangular sandwiches, Ettie spotted a bowl of soft candies. She leaned over and popped one into her mouth.

"Try a cupcake, Ettie."

"I might when I finish this."

"They're moist and the frosting is good too."

Ettie took a cupcake and was just about to take a bite when she heard raised voices. She turned to see Marlene talking to Dawn.

"I thought this might happen," Elsa-May whispered.

After Ettie had taken a bite of cake, she looked around for Kelly and saw him walking toward Marlene. "Mmm," she said, "the cake *is* good."

"I told you."

Elsa-May and Ettie continued to watch as Kelly said a few quiet words to Marlene and then led Dawn out of the room.

"It was a bad idea for her to come," Elsa-May said.

"Why shouldn't she come to her friend's funeral?"

"Because it was obvious that Marlene's angry with her, that's why. You don't have to be a genius to figure that out."

When Kelly came back inside, he was alone. Ettie

continued to watch while Kelly headed back over to Marlene.

"I'm going to see if I can hear what they say."

"Okay, but don't get too close."

Ettie moved over until she could hear.

"What are you doing about the diamond she stole from me?" Marlene hissed.

"She has a note from your father saying it was a gift, in thanks for all her attention and service. I read it myself and it's your father's handwriting."

"Before that, there was a verbal contract between my mother and myself where she said she'd give it to me. I was their only child."

"You'll have to take that up with a lawyer."

"That woman probably forced him to write that note. He was old and stupid and didn't know what he was doing."

"When was the last time you spoke to your father?"

"I couldn't say."

"It seems reasonable to me that your father gave the diamond to the woman who looked after him as a token of his appreciation, since you were no longer around."

"I was busy and anyway, I'm his only child and I found his will in his paperwork and everything was left to me."

"As I said, that's something you'll have to take up with a lawyer."

"Yeah, but they cost money. Why should I have to

go to the expense of court and all that? You should just give it back to me because it's mine! She'd give it back if you said to. She's only hanging onto it because she thinks she can."

Marlene was raising her voice again and Ettie was feeling a little sorry for Detective Kelly.

"I should just go and get it back from her myself."

"That wouldn't be a good idea," Kelly said calmly.

"Yeah? Well isn't possession nine-tenths of the law?"

"I'm not a lawyer, but I'd advise you not to try getting it back any other way but through the courts, or else you could find yourself facing criminal charges."

"It's my diamond! It was my mother's and she wanted me to have it!"

Now she'd grown so loud that everyone was staring at her. Her husband hurried over to her and whispered something in her ear, which sent her storming outside.

"I'm sorry about that, Detective," Marlene's husband said, "My wife is upset because we're renewing our vows soon for our twentieth wedding anniversary. She wanted the diamond to put into a new ring. I could never have afforded a diamond of that size and that's all she ever wanted."

"Is that right?"

"Yes. I'm only a labourer and things are tough because I've got a bad back now and Marlene has never worked. At least we can sell her old man's house now and have a bit left over once the mortgage is paid up.

Although the realtor reckons we won't get much, with the murder and all."

Kelly nodded. "It's an emotional time. Funerals are hard on close relatives."

Ettie wondered how long ago they had planned the renewing of their vows. Would Marlene have killed her own father while hunting down the diamond? Could she have gone to her father's house and asked for the diamond and when he said it wasn't there, she could've thought he was lying and then hunted everywhere for it. And, when he tried to stop her tearing the place apart...."

"Did you hear all that?"

Ettie jumped when she saw Detective Kelly was right beside her. "Yes, well, some of it. Interesting about her wanting the diamond for the ring. And she'd have been furious about the housekeeper owning the diamond if that's all Marlene had ever wanted, like her husband said."

Ettie knew that Marlene had moved onto Kelly's list of suspects.

"Did Jazeel tell you that it was Dawn who asked him to look after him while she was away on vacation?" Ettie asked.

"Yes, she mentioned that and that helps his case, but we still haven't looked at that CCTV footage."

Ettie hoped Jazeel would soon be in the clear. "Try a cupcake, Detective. They're delicious."

CHAPTER 14

THE NEXT MORNING AFTER BREAKFAST, Ettie and Elsa-May were sitting in their living room.

Elsa-May knitted while Ettie worked on a sampler.

Ettie broke the silence. "I didn't like that funeral."

"I know. You've told me a dozen times this morning already," Elsa-May said, shaking her head.

"I think Kelly thinks that Marlene might have killed her father to get the diamond. And I wonder how much money she'll get from the sale of Alfie's house."

"That's just speculation."

"I know, but Kelly always says that in most murder cases it's someone the victim knows, and it's normally a family member," Ettie said. "And anything to do with money is a strong motive, too."

"Don't forget the man that just got out of prison."

"I'm not. Kelly hasn't mentioned him again."

Elsa-May said, "He didn't mention him yesterday, but he'll be finding him and interviewing him. And that man is not someone we can talk with, and if you want to find him, you're going to have to do all that on your own. He might have murdered someone and Alfie knew about it and then he killed Alfie."

"Also, let's not forget the drug dealers," Ettie said.

"They weren't drug dealers, they were drug buyers."

"That's right. Well, whatever they were, they could've killed Alfie too." Ettie sighed. "We're developing a long list. Marlene, the drug buyers, and the man who was just released from prison."

"Bruno Gillespie."

"Yes, that's the one. Let's try to figure this thing out. We're two intelligent women, so we should be able to work out who killed Uncle Alfie."

"You've got that half right," Elsa-May murmured.

Ettie was used to those kinds of comments. She nearly said, *I'm sorry you don't think you qualify*. It was less effort to pretend she wasn't listening. She pushed her needle into the fabric to keep her place and put her sampler on the couch next to her.

"Uncle Alfie was stabbed, and don't they say women don't usually kill by stabbing? They use less violent methods of killing such as poison, or... something like that," Ettie said.

"I hear what you're saying, but she's not an ordinary woman. I could see Marlene stabbing someone."

THE AMISH CAT CAPER

"Let's rule her out for the moment. I can't see her killing her only immediate family member."

"Okay, continue. Let's hear it. Keep going." Elsa-May continued her knitting.

"Now we come to the drug buyers. If Alphie had what they wanted why would they stab him? There was no microphone or amplifier at the house, so they must've taken it. So, in my mind that clears them."

"Well, not necessarily. If they were on drugs they might have become irrational."

"*Nee*, it just doesn't seem logical."

"Again, you're expecting people on drugs to be logical?"

Ettie continued, "They probably weren't under the influence at the time because they'd gone back to Joe demanding money."

"In a violent manner. Don't forget they beat him up."

Ettie clicked her tongue. "It must've been the man who just got out of prison. What we need to find out is what evidence Uncle Alfie was keeping about him, and why."

"Sounds easy enough. We'll just go down to the graveyard and ask him, shall we?"

"We might not need to, Elsa-May, we might not need to." Ettie pushed herself to her feet and went to the front door and pulled on her shawl.

"Where are you going?"

"I'm going to talk to Jazeel. I think he knows more than he thinks he does."

Elsa-May frowned and looked at Ettie over the top of her knitting glasses.

Ettie put her hands on her hips and stared at Elsa-May. "Coming?"

Pushing out her lips, Elsa-May said, "I suppose so."

When they got into the taxi, Ettie gave the driver Molly's address.

"Do you think Jazeel's going to be at Molly's *haus?*" Elsa-May asked her.

"*Jah,* I do."

"I suppose it wouldn't hurt to try there first."

When the taxi turned into the street, Ettie saw Jazeel's buggy tied up in front of Molly's place. "See?" she said to Elsa-May.

"Good guess."

They knocked on the door and Jazeel opened the door and ushered them in quickly, before Tom could escape. When they were inside, Molly released Tom and he slinked into the kitchen.

The sisters accepted an offer of hot tea, and sat in the living room.

When Molly came back with the tea, Ettie said to Jazeel, "How long ago did Alfie tell you about…"

"Bruno Gillespie," Elsa-May said, filling in when Ettie hesitated.

"*Denke,* Elsa-May."

"It would be a few years ago now." He rubbed his chin. "My Aunt Emily was still alive and she won the competition around the same time."

"The one where she won the money to buy the diamond?" Ettie asked.

"That's the story," he said.

Elsa-May leaned forward and picked up her tea cup. "Do you mean you didn't believe your Aunt Emily won a competition?"

He hunched his shoulders. "It could've been true, but it struck me that a diamond was a weird thing to buy with the money."

"Why?" Elsa-May asked.

"I don't know. Don't listen to me. I suppose if I won so much money I might go out and buy something impractical as well, but Aunt Emily was a sensible person."

"Did you ever see it?" Ettie asked.

"*Jah.* Aunt Emily never had it off her neck. It didn't look real if you ask me. It wasn't a regular diamond. It was pink."

"That is unusual," Elsa-May said. "I didn't know they came in pink."

"Why are you so interested in the diamond, Ettie?"

"I'm not. I was asking about Bruno Gillespie. Now I'm thinking about something else. Jazeel, do you know what the competition was? Who held it—that kind of thing?"

"No one ever said—not to me anyway."

At that moment, they heard a car outside. Jazeel stood and looked out the window.

"It's Detective Kelly."

"I hope it's good news," Molly said.

"Grab Tom, Molly, so I can open the door."

Molly went to grab Tom who was now sitting on top of the cat carrier.

"Okay I've got him," Molly called out as soon as Tom was restrained.

Jazeel opened the door for the detective and Kelly walked inside. Jazeel closed the door behind him.

Molly released her hold on Tom, who continued to sit atop his carrier.

Kelly looked over and saw Ettie and Elsa-May. "Everyone's here, I see." Then he saw Molly at the side of the room. "Hello, Ms. Miller." His eyes fell to Tom and he walked over. "And who do we have here?" He put his hand out to touch the cat, and everyone froze, too stunned to warn the detective. Tom sat there, perfectly still, and let Kelly stroke his fur. "What a lovely cat. What's his name?"

"This is Tom."

"He's so friendly."

"Is he purring?" When Molly leaned down to hear if the rumbling was indeed Tom's purring, the cat turned around and hissed at her.

"Yes, he's purring," Kelly said as he swung around to face a wide-eyed Jazeel. "Now, I have good news for you, Jazeel. We have CCTV footage of you getting on a bus, which puts you on a bus at the same time the coroner estimates the time of Alfred Graber's death. That puts you in the clear."

"How in the world did you pat the cat?" Jazeel asked.

Kelly stared at Jazeel. "Did you hear what I said?"

Jazeel blinked a couple times. "I'm in the clear? Is that what you're saying?"

"Yes. Your charges have been dropped."

"Thank you, Detective, that's such good news. What a relief! Sit with us and have tea."

"I don't have time today, sorry. I have to get right back to the station, but I wanted to deliver this news in person."

"Thank you." Jazeel nodded and shook Kelly's hand.

"How are your investigations going?" Ettie asked as she stood up and started walking toward him.

"Fine, fine. We're following up leads."

Elsa-May called out from the couch. "Jazeel's got interesting information you might want to hear."

Kelly whipped his head around to look at Jazeel. "You do?"

"I don't know if it's interesting or not, but I was just saying how I never heard what competition Aunt Emily won the diamond in, and I always doubted it was a real diamond because it was pink."

"Pink?"

"Yes."

"No one mentioned that to me before."

"Wasn't the housekeeper wearing it at the funeral?" Ettie asked.

"No, and that's good because that would've most likely started World War Three." He patted Tom again, and then he said, "I've got to check on a few things." Kelly hurried out the door while Molly once more held onto Tom to stop him from running out.

"You were such a good boy, Tom."

Tom yowled at her and ran to the front door, which was now closed. He sat there staring at the door.

"Looks like Kelly's made a friend," Ettie said to Elsa-May as she sat back down.

Elsa-May shook her head. "If I hadn't seen it with my own eyes I would never have believed it. He never pats Snowy."

"He must be a cat-lover. After this, we're heading to the library," Ettie whispered to Elsa-May.

"I guessed as much."

CHAPTER 15

*E*TTIE AND ELSA-MAY walked into the library and headed to one of the computers.

"You'll have to do it, Ettie. I left my glasses at home. I didn't know we'd be coming here. You only said we were off to Molly's *haus*."

"Plans changed." Ettie sat behind the computer and Elsa-May pulled a chair over next to her. "Firstly I'll look up Bruno Gillespie."

"Is Bruno a real name, Ettie, or is it short for something?"

"It's a real name. Remember Bruno Polk, who fixed the buggies when we were young girls?"

"That's right. He had long black and white hair. Salt-and-pepper hair, or so I've heard it called."

"*Jah*. Now don't distract me. I haven't done this in awhile." Ettie looked through the search choices after she typed in Bruno Gillespie's name.

"What does it say?"

"He was convicted on two counts of theft. Now this information is going back five years; that must be when he went to jail."

"Now look up about a large pink diamond and see if any were stolen before then."

"Okay." After the search came up, Ettie said, "I found something. A large pink diamond was stolen from Brussels, just two months before Bruno's trial."

"Could that be it? Could Alfie have been looking after the diamond?"

Ettie was still reading. "It says here that pink diamonds can be worth hundreds of times more than the same size clear diamond."

"Hundreds of times? Not twice as much, but hundreds?"

"That's what it says here in this news article."

"I just asked you if you think that Alfie and Emily were looking after the diamond for Bruno?"

"It's possible."

"But why would Alfie give the diamond away to the housekeeper? He would've known the man would be coming back to get it."

"Uncle Alfie was a sick man. What if he was losing his mind and he'd come to believe the story that Emily won money and bought it, just like they told their daughter?"

Ettie pulled a face. "I don't think he lost his mind.

He'd have to be really far gone to give the diamond away."

Elsa-May sighed. "I suppose you're right. Unless the housekeeper forged that note she got with the diamond."

"*Nee.* Don't you remember? Jazeel was there when he gave her the diamond and Uncle Alfie must've written the nice note to her afterward."

"And just as well he did or it's possible no one might have believed the housekeeper that it had been given to her."

"We'll have to find out if the diamond is the same diamond as the one that was stolen from Brussels. Here it is on the screen. Can you see it?"

Elsa-May squinted. "*Jah,* I can see it."

"It says here it's a third of an inch across and it says it's two karats. And five years ago it was worth over one million dollars."

"*Nee!*" Elsa-May gasped.

"*Jah.* We have to tell Kelly."

"Okay. You do that."

Ettie turned to face her sister. "Won't you come with me?"

"Didn't he tell us to keep out of things."

"He knows us well enough to know that we won't."

Elsa-May sighed. "I'll come with you as long as you do all the talking."

. . .

An hour later, they were sitting in front of Detective Kelly.

"I must admit, I was thinking along the same lines as both of you."

Elsa-May leaned forward. "You mean, as Ettie?"

Kelly raised an eyebrow and continued, "That diamond was stolen from Brussels. I know the one you mean because it was all over the news at the time. But that stone was recovered six months after the robbery."

Elsa-May dug her sister in the ribs. "You should've searched that on the Internet, Ettie. It would've been there. Why didn't you think of that before you came and bothered Detective Kelly?"

Ettie looked at her sister and her mouth fell open. "Why didn't *you* think of that, Elsa-May?"

Kelly chuckled. "It was a good line of thought, although probably a tad far-fetched. Bruno Gillespie has never left the country. We know that for a fact. I must say though, Mrs. Smith, Mrs. Lutz, the diamond hasn't been sitting right with me along. I see you Amish as plain-living people. Even though Alfred and his wife had left the community, as far as I could see from their house, they still lived modestly. So, what would they want with a large diamond?" He shook his head. "Something is wrong there. Since the diamond has caused some drama, I've got two men looking into the competition that Emily Graber had reportedly won. So far, they've come up empty handed. As far as Bruno

Gillespie having any involvement in Alfred's death, he's got a solid alibi for that whole day."

Ettie's shoulders drooped. "What about the pink diamond being so valuable? Wouldn't it have been worth more than twenty thousand back then even if it was a colourless diamond?"

"Ettie found out that a pink diamond would be worth so much more," Elsa-May said.

"And that's why I've asked Alfred's housekeeper if we can kindly examine the diamond. We'll have it appraised, and then we'll see if that helps us move the case forward. It's my job to look at every angle of this case."

"And what other angles are you looking at?" Ettie asked.

"I don't think that there's anything you can help me with this time, Mrs. Smith. I have appreciated your help before, though, when I've had issues in the past related to the Amish community."

"Could Gillespie have paid someone to kill Alfred?" Elsa-May asked.

Ettie stared her sister. "I thought you wanted to keep out of this."

"I'm just asking a question, Ettie."

Both sisters then stared at the detective, waiting for a response.

"It is possible, but then again, he could've done that from prison at any time if he'd wanted to. Firstly, we'd have to establish if he had a motive; examining the diamond might give us a bit more information. That's what we're hoping."

"When will you know about the diamond?"

"We've got an appraiser looking at it tomorrow, so we'll know more by tomorrow evening." Kelly stood up. "Now if you'll excuse me, ladies, I've got some appointments to get to."

CHAPTER 16

"*T*HANKS FOR THROWING me under the bus in there," Ettie said, glaring at Elsa-May once they were outside the station.

"What do you mean? Kelly said he was thinking along the same lines as you that something's not right with that diamond."

Ettie sighed. "*Jah,* but I was wrong. I felt such a fool. That pink diamond was found."

Elsa-May gleefully added, "And Bruno Gillespie has never been out of the country."

Ettie huffed.

"Don't worry, the police have access to all the information that tells him these things, but do you know what we have that they don't?"

"*Nee,* what?"

"We aren't police and people talk to us because they think we are a couple of silly old ladies."

Ettie giggled.

"Let's go up the road to your favorite coffee shop and I'll buy you lunch."

"Really? You'll buy?" Ettie asked.

"*Jah*."

"You never pay for lunch, or anything."

"I am today."

Elsa-May and Ettie walked arm-in-arm two blocks up the road to their special place, a shop that made delicious cakes and food.

As they walked in the door and stood looking at all the cakes in the glass display case, Elsa-May said, "I normally let you pay because you've got a lot more money than me."

"That's okay. I don't mind. What else will I do with it?" All Ettie's children who had stayed within the community were financially stable, so she had no need to help them out. Two of her daughters had left the community years ago. One was doing okay, and the other, she had neither seen nor heard from in years. Ettie figured if she hadn't heard from that daughter, she must be doing okay too.

"What will you have Ettie?"

"Um, are we having lunch or a snack?"

"Whatever you like."

"What time is it?" Ettie asked.

"It's twelve, but don't go by time. If you're hungry eat, and if you aren't, then don't."

"I'm never really hungry."

"That's why you have no meat on your bones. Hurry up, the lady's waiting to take your order."

Ettie ordered a salad sandwich and a piece of chocolate cake to follow it with, and Elsa-May ordered the same. They sat at one of the small wooden tables and waited for their food.

"What's our next step?" Ettie asked her sister.

Elsa-May scratched her face. "I was thinking we might visit the housekeeper, but if the police have the diamond, they've been in contact with her so maybe we should keep away."

"What about the whole drug deal gone wrong? Do you think one of those men might have done it to Uncle Alfie?"

"Would they have had to? He was a sick old man. If someone came into his house to take something, he wouldn't have been able to stop them. They would've walked in, taken it, and walked out. Easy!"

"I suppose so."

The waitress brought their food over.

"*Denke*, Elsa-May, this looks good. We won't have to eat dinner tonight."

Elsa-May picked up half a sandwich. "Are we missing something? Maybe it's someone else entirely."

"Who?"

"I don't know."

Ettie took a bite of her sandwich while wondering again, *who killed Uncle Alfie?*

"Ettie, why don't we visit Marlene today?"

After she'd swallowed her mouthful, Ettie said, "We could do that, but would she know anything? She hadn't seen her father for years."

Elsa-May raised her eyebrows.

"Oh, you're thinking she might have had something to do with his death?"

"That's what we thought at the beginning. Remember?"

"*Jah*, that's right. Okay let's do it. I remember at the funeral her husband was telling Detective Kelly she didn't work, so we know she'd most likely be home."

"We just need to find out where she lives, and on the way there we'll figure out what questions to ask her." Elsa-May munched into her sandwich.

Ettie nodded. "I just hope she doesn't live too far away."

Elsa-May waved the waitress over and asked to borrow their phone book. When she brought it to the table, Elsa-May looked in the book.

"You remember her married name?" Ettie asked.

"I do. I remember it from the funeral. It was Clark. Her name is Marlene Clark. I remember thinking that the three middle letters of her surname shared three letters with her first name, but the outside letters were different."

Ettie shook her head. "I've got no idea how your brain works to even think of such a thing."

Elsa-May smiled as she leafed through the phone book. "His name is Max, which could be short for something, but hopefully it still starts with an M. Here we go, 'M & M Clark.' I hope that's them, and they only live about ten minutes from here."

"Good. We can go by taxi."

"I only hope it's them."

"Are there any other M & M Clarks?"

Elsa-May looked down at the page again. *"Nee."*

"There's a good chance it's them. Shall we ask for pen and paper to write down the address?"

"Nee. I've already got it up here." Elsa-May tapped on her forehead.

CHAPTER 17

*E*TTIE AND ELSA-MAY got out of the taxi and knocked on the door of the house they hoped was Marlene's. It was a small red brick house with a single garage to one side.

While they waited at the front door, Ettie whispered, "There's no garden; there's just grass."

"Not everyone wants a garden. They're a lot of upkeep." Elsa-May picked lint off Ettie's black shawl and Ettie pushed her hand away.

Ettie said, "She doesn't work outside the home, so she could easily—"

"Sh, Ettie."

The door opened slightly and, sure enough, Marlene looked out. When a look of recognition spread across her face, she opened it wider. "Oh, it's you."

"Yes. It's us," Elsa-May said. "Ettie Smith and I'm

Elsa-May Lutz. You might not remember us from when you were in the community, but we remember you."

She looked past them. "Are you by yourselves?"

"Yes."

"Do you want to come in?"

"Yes please."

She opened the door wide and stood back to let them through. Then she showed them to a small sunroom. "Can I get you anything?"

"No, thank you. We've just had lunch."

"Ettie and I thought we'd come and see how you're coping now."

She nodded. "I'm doing okay. It was a nasty shock, but I've got a lawyer on the job."

"On the job of what?"

"Getting the diamond back."

Ettie and Elsa-May looked at one another.

"We're here to see how you're coping after the death of your father," Ettie said.

"Oh, yes, much better thanks. It's nice of you to stop by. No one else has bothered."

"And you hadn't seen your father for many years?" Elsa-May asked.

"Yes, that's true. We had a few words after my mother died, and I said if he wanted to talk to me again he'd need to apologize, but he never did."

"Can I ask what you had an argument about?" Ettie asked.

"We had so many it's hard to say. I don't think there

was just one thing. The last straw that did it for me..." Marlene took a deep breath before she continued, "It was when my mother died and my father didn't give me anything of hers. He said I'd left the community and I didn't deserve anything."

"Hadn't he left by then too?"

Marlene nodded and leaned back in the couch crossing one leg over the other. "My parents left when I was a young girl and now I'm fifty two. He said he was thinking of going back and I should too. I was married to Max, and I knew Max wouldn't want to join the Amish and I only had bad memories of it, so I was certainly never going back there."

"That's a shame," Elsa-May said.

"Two of my daughters feel the same way, unfortunately."

"Yeah, well, anyway, my mother didn't have much and I just wanted some keepsake."

"Did you end up getting anything?" Elsa-May asked.

"Nothing. He said I wasn't welcome because I hardly visited them. I told him I didn't have a car. Back then Max and I only had one car between us and he needed it for his work. We still only have one car, since I don't have a job."

"What kind of work does he do?"

"He's in liquor sales and he needs his vehicle for that because he has to visit customers."

"This might seem like a strange question Marlene, but.... Um..." Elsa-May shook her head.

"What were you going to ask, Elsa-May?"

"I've forgotten. Oh, that's right. I was going to ask you if you remember that competition that your mother won money in."

"I remember her winning the competition, but I don't know anything about it. Back then I was only seeing them every few months. I knew it caused more problems between my parents because my father wanted to do other things with that money. *Mamm* said it was hers and she was going to give it to me if they went back to the community. That's what she said." Marlene straightened her back. "Are you sure I can't get you a cup of tea, maybe, or coffee?"

"I would like tea please and Ettie would like one too."

Marlene smiled. "I won't be long."

When she was out of the room, Ettie whispered, "Why are you talking for me?"

"You would've made a big fuss how you didn't want one. If we drink tea we'll be able to find out more because we'll get to stay longer."

"Okay, but don't do it again. It makes me feel like a child."

Elsa-May narrowed her eyes. "There are bigger things at stake here than your feelings."

Ettie breathed out heavily, doing her best to ignore her irritation with her sister.

Marlene came back and sat down. "I've just put the kettle on. It won't be long." She folded her arms in front of her and leaned back. "It was a last parting jab at me that my father gave the diamond to that silly old cow of a housekeeper. I would've done things for them if I'd lived closer, and if they had been nicer to me."

"They?" Ettie asked.

"My mother and my father. Neither of them was all that nice to me even though I was their only child. Most single children are spoiled, but not me. They never really cared about me. I was just a bother to them."

"Marlene, I don't think that's true."

"You weren't there, Elsa-May. No one knew what they were really like. They were all smiles when they had visitors and when they were out amongst other people, but at home they argued and quarrelled. It wasn't nice to be around. Neither of them was happy. I don't think they wanted to be married to each other."

"And yet they remained together when they left the community," Ettie pointed out.

"Yeah, well, they'd probably grown used to each other by then. Or it might have been a case of better the devil you know than the one you don't. Anyway, my father probably wanted my mother to stick around so she could be an unpaid housekeeper, and to cook for him."

Ettie looked at Elsa-May to see what she thought.

"That's the kettle." Marlene jumped up when whistling came from the kitchen.

"She's not a happy person," Ettie whispered.

"We knew that before we came. What we need to do is find out something we don't know." Elsa-May gave a sharp nod of her head.

"Do you want some help in there?" Ettie called out to Marlene.

"No, I'm fine. I won't be a minute."

Marlene came back with a tray of tea and chocolate cookies.

"This looks lovely," Ettie said wondering how she'd get through everything since they'd only just had lunch, including the large slab of chocolate cake she'd eaten.

Elsa-May nibbled on a chocolate cookie while Marlene poured the tea.

"My mother liked hot tea. That was one thing we shared. We would often sit up at night and she'd tell me stories of when she was a girl. She'd had a good childhood growing up in a family of fifteen children. There was always someone to play with and she was able to tell me many funny stories of the trouble they often found themselves in."

"Ettie and I come from a large family as well."

"Elsa-May was the oldest girl and that's why she's so bossy," Ettie added, which made Marlene laugh.

"I suppose there are disadvantages to larger families too," Marlene said.

"Did your parents have many *Englischer* friends?" Elsa-May asked when she had stopped glaring at Ettie.

"Not many at all. They didn't go out much. The

man next door seemed to come in a lot, and one or two other people visited, but that was about it."

"If I remember correctly, they moved to that house when they left the community and they never moved again?" Elsa-May asked.

"That's right. They had a farm and it was too much work, and I wasn't born a boy and had no interest in working the land, so they sold the farm and that's when they decided to leave the community too. I forgot about that. My parents wanted a boy."

Ettie pulled a face at Elsa-May for reminding Marlene of something else to be cross about.

After Elsa-May slurped her tea loudly, setting Ettie's nerves on edge, she moved in her seat and said to Marlene, "Who do you think killed your father?"

Marlene's gaze flickered to the ceiling. "I'll leave that up to the detectives," she finally said.

"Surely you've got some theories," Ettie said studying her for any sign of nervousness.

"I think it was just a home invasion. Anyone could've done it."

"It's an unusual thing to die that way. He was an old man and he wasn't well. If anyone wanted something they could've taken it. There was no need to kill him."

"I wonder why the next door neighbor didn't hear anything."

"He didn't?"

"The main detective said he didn't," Marlene said.

Elsa-May said, "No guns were fired. They might not have made a loud noise."

Marlene shrugged. "I guess."

"Why? Did your father and the neighbor have a falling out over something?"

"My father was often arguing with people. He wasn't an easy man to get along with. That's why my mother was sad all the time."

Ettie was starting to get a different picture of Uncle Alfie as she thought back to his wife, Emily. She recalled that she couldn't remember ever seeing Emily smile after she was married to Alfie.

"What things would he argue about with people?"

"Why are you asking all these questions?"

"My sister and I are trying to piece things together—"

Elsa-May butted in, "To see if your father really gave his housekeeper the diamond."

Marlene's face lighted up. "That's so nice of you. I've never had anyone on my side apart from Max. Normally no one cares about me. That detective certainly didn't care. He just kept telling me he couldn't do anything to get it back for me because he wasn't a lawyer. But I don't have the money for court."

Ettie nodded.

When they finished their tea, Ettie helped Marlene wash the teacups in the kitchen. Then the sisters borrowed Marlene's phone to call a taxi. When it arrived and the sisters were inside, Elsa-May said, "Well, that was a complete waste of time."

"It was your idea," Ettie shot back.

"Was it?"

Ettie nodded. "Anyway, it wasn't a complete waste of time. I'd always had the picture in my mind of Alfie being how he was when he was younger. He was only a couple of years younger than me and we went to the same *schul*. It was a one-room building back then. From what Marlene said, Alfie had changed considerably."

"I was thinking that too. And I think Marlene's right about her mother never being happy."

"That's right; that's how I remember her."

ETTIE AND ELSA-MAY got back home to find a note on their door.

"Open it, Ettie."

Ettie carefully unfolded it. "It's from Molly and Jazeel. They're inviting us to Molly's house on Tuesday night. They're having quite a crowd, she says. That's after their rededication on Sunday. I wonder if they're doing that so everyone will know they're a couple."

"They saw us this morning and never mentioned a thing."

"Perhaps they decided it since."

"They must've."

CHAPTER 18

THE FOLLOWING AFTERNOON, Ettie and Elsa-May were just sitting down to shell peas for dinner when they heard knocking on their door.

"Who could that be?" Elsa-May asked.

Snowy yapped and bounded to the door.

"I'd say that would be Detective Kelly. You should put Snowy outside."

Ettie went to the door while Elsa-May locked Snowy outside because the dog loved to paw at Kelly's leg.

"It is you," Ettie said when she opened the door to see Kelly standing there. "Come in."

Kelly walked in. "Ah good. You've got the hound locked outside."

"Do you have news?" Ettie asked.

"Yes."

"Well, sit down and let's hear it," Elsa-May said.

"Would you like—"

"I'm fine thank you," Kelly said cutting Ettie off. He sat down on a chair in the living room and waited until Ettie and Elsa-May were seated. Then he said, "It's about the diamond."

The sister leaned forward, and said as one, "Yes?"

"First of all, it wasn't a pink diamond after all. It's a dirty pale yellowish color."

"So it's not worth a lot?"

"Not that much and it's got big black inclusions within the stone, bringing the value down even further."

"Did you find out if there was a competition?"

"We haven't been able to find a competition and we've got bank account records, both Alfred's and his late wife's, and we can't find a record of that amount going into either of their accounts."

"What's the diamond worth?"

"It might have been sold for around twenty thousand. Not saying it was worth that, but that's what they might've paid. We've got no reason to believe that there's any connection linking the diamond to the murder, and we can't find that Bruno Gillespie had anything to do with the murder."

"Well, what evidence did Uncle Alfie have about him?"

"We don't know that he had anything. All we've got is Jazeel's word for that, and he's going by something Alfie told him, which might not have even been true."

Elsa-May drew her eyebrows together. "Then why say it if it wasn't true?"

"Mrs. Lutz, you come from a place in your head where you think everyone tells the truth. I'm here to tell you that that's simply not so. The man might have been boasting to his nephew to look like a hero, or so he'd appear larger-than-life in his nephew's eyes."

"Where does that leave us?" Ettie asked.

"We can forget that the diamond had anything to do with his death. We're still investigating it though, but I figure it'll only lead us to a dead end. Don't worry, we'll leave no stone unturned and we will find out who did this to the poor old man."

"How about the drug dealers? How are you getting on with investigating them?" Ettie asked.

"She means the people who bought the drugs from Joe Mulligan."

"We're fairly certain we've located them. We just need Mulligan to give us a positive ID. Then we'll bring them in for questioning."

"You know, I might have a hot cup of tea if you don't mind," Kelly said.

Elsa-May pushed herself to her feet. "Coming up."

"That cat you patted yesterday at Molly Miller's house..."

"Yes. I remember."

"He's wild."

His eyes opened wide. "He didn't appear to be."

"He doesn't like anyone, not even his owner."

He chuckled. "I noticed everyone was looking at me strangely when I patted him."

"Well, that's why. He always attacks people. Except you, for some reason. And he tried to follow you when you left."

"I have a fondness for cats."

"Do you own any pets?"

Detective Kelly shook his head. "In my line of work it wouldn't be fair. I'm hardly ever home."

While Ettie sat and chatted with the detective, she wondered whom else she could find out about. "Have you talked to Dave, Uncle Alfie's neighbor, lately?"

"Not in the last couple of days. Why?"

"He didn't see anyone coming or going the night Alfie was murdered?"

"Not a thing. He was fast asleep."

CHAPTER 19

JAZEEL QUICKLY SLIPPED into the house before Tom could run away.

"Thanks for coming early to help," I said as he gave me a quick kiss on the cheek.

"How are you feeling today, Molly?"

"I'm fine. I'm looking forward to having everyone over here."

"It was good of you to invite Max and Marlene."

"Well, I thought it wouldn't hurt since Marlene is your cousin. She's part of the family. I remember her a little bit from my days in the community, but she was a lot younger than I."

The bishop had told us we could marry in two months. We had decided we would move into my house after the wedding and then Jazeel would lease his, since my house was on a much nicer street. Jazeel said he'd build a big enclosure in the back yard for Tom to roam free in.

"Could you help by chopping the parsley finely?"

"Sure."

Every time I saw a large knife I was reminded of Jazeel's Uncle Alfie, whom I'd known as a girl.

Days later.

WHEN EVERYONE HAD ARRIVED at my lovely dinner party, the first I was to have with Jazeel after we'd officially returned to the community, Ettie stood up and clapped her hands. I stared at her wondering what was going on. This was my dinner!

Ettie began, "I'm glad everyone's here together tonight and remembering Alfie. Marlene, you were very upset by the way your parents always treated you, and made you feel that they wanted you to have been born a boy."

A few sniggers were heard.

"It's true," Marlene said in a large voice.

"You were also upset that your father never let you have any keepsakes from your mother. And when you found out he gave the one thing you were hoping for to the housekeeper you became enraged."

"I didn't kill him," Marlene said.

I looked at Ettie, wondering what she was doing. All

I'd wanted was to have a nice get-together. I'd even locked Tom in the spare bedroom so no one would scare him. I'd gone to a lot of trouble.

Ettie's face scrunched and the wrinkles in her face deepened as she turned and looked right at Marlene's husband, Max.

"That's right Marlene, you didn't kill your father, because you didn't have to. Your husband did that for you," Ettie said.

Max jumped to his feet. "I did not! What are you saying?"

"Ettie, why are you saying these things?" Marlene stood and grabbed hold of her husband's arm.

Ettie paced across the floor in the opposite direction from my guests, and then she swung around to look back at Marlene. "When I was in your kitchen the other day helping you with the dishes, I spotted that you had the largest knife missing from your wooden block of knives. And not long after, I found that very knife hidden at your house. I took it and handed it to the police. It was tested, and showed positive with your father's blood."

Marlene looked at her husband with an open mouth.

"It's a lie," he said. "It's all a lie."

"What part is a lie?" Ettie asked. "You listened to Marlene tell you how horrible her father was for years. You were just being a good husband when you snuffed out the source of Marlene's misery."

"I never… I don't know what you're talking about," Max said to Ettie.

"How long has that knife been missing, Marlene?"

Marlene opened her mouth to speak but no words came out.

"Don't listen to her, Marlene."

"The knife… "

"She's lying about the knife," Max said.

"You said you had it in the garage and you were sharpening it."

Max nodded. "That's right and it's still there."

"What knife did you find at my house, Ettie?"

"I found it covered in blood, in your trash can outside. I saw it when I was throwing the scraps from the cake into the bin."

"That's a lie," Max blurted out.

"It tested positive for Alfie's blood and Max's fingerprints were on the handle."

Max shouted. "That's a lie. I wore gloves…"

Everyone gasped and stared at Max.

"I didn't do it," he said loudly, and then he leaped up and ran out the front door.

I ran to the front door and saw Max being taken away in handcuffs by police who must've been hiding in the bushes. I looked at Ettie. "Is it true, Ettie?"

Ettie looked at Marlene, who was now standing beside her. "You had no idea?"

She shook her head. "Why would he?"

I was right next to them when I said, "Perhaps he

wanted the diamond for you, and the money you could get for the house."

"I never wanted anything that way," Marlene said. "Now I've got no one."

"You've got your cousins," I said putting my arm around her shoulder. I knew what it was like to have no one. "Jazeel's your cousin and I'll be your cousin too when Jazeel and I get married."

Marlene gave a tiny smile, which told me she appreciated my words.

The detective walked into the house and said, "Thank you for your help, Mrs. Smith."

"You knew all along?" Marlene looked from Detective Kelly to Ettie.

"We put our heads together and came up with a plan."

"Did you really find a knife, Ettie?" Marlene asked her.

Ettie shook her head. "I saw that the one knife was missing, and I described the kind of knives they were to the detective after I estimated the size of the larger one going by the gap in the wooden block. He said that was roughly the same size as the murder weapon, and that knife wasn't found at the scene."

"I'm sorry, Mrs. Clark," Detective Kelly said. "This must've come as a nasty shock.

"It has. I can't believe he would've done something like that." She looked up at Detective Kelly. "What'll happen to him?"

Kelly scratched his cheek. "He might not get bail considering the violent nature of the crime and his public confession. He'll go before a judge in the morning and if he gets bail, he'll be back home with you tomorrow until the trial."

"And if he doesn't?"

"He'll stay in prison until the trial."

"Would you like me to go with you tomorrow?" I offered, having just gone through the same thing when Jazeel had been accused of Uncle Alfie's murder.

"Yes, I would," Marlene answered. "I'll fetch you first thing in the morning."

"I'll be waiting."

The whole event had ruined my first get together as a couple with Jazeel. One by one, people made excuses to leave, and I could hardly blame them. We'd have another after our wedding.

I looked over at Jazeel, who'd been sitting quietly on the couch watching the whole scene play out. I walked over to him while Ettie and Elsa-May comforted Marlene.

"You must be feeling dreadful."

"I'm glad the police got the right man, but I'm upset that it happened at all. The father that Marlene talks about is not the same Uncle Alfie that I knew."

I sat down next to him and took hold of his hand.

His blue eyes crinkled at the corners when he looked into my eyes. "Now I've got you to share the good times and the bad times."

"I'll always be around to help you through anything."

He shook his head. "I was certain it was Bruno Gillespie who killed him."

"*Jah.* I wonder what Uncle Alfie had on Bruno. Do you think we'll ever find out?"

"I hope we do."

"Have you ever asked Marlene?"

"*Nee.* And now's not the time. I'm sorry your dinner is ruined."

When I looked up, there was only Ettie, Elsa-May, Detective Kelly, and Marlene left. "There'll be a lot more food for the six of us." I walked over to Detective Kelly. "Would you care to stay and have something to eat? We've plenty here."

"I'd love to, but I have to get back and conduct an interview." His eyes swept across the table. "It all looks delicious."

"How about just a chicken leg? I'll wrap it to go."

He nodded. "That would be lovely. Thank you."

I wrapped a large piece of chicken for the detective and then he was on his way, leaving just the five of us. Marlene was sitting at the table, quietly sobbing.

"Would you like to stay here with me tonight, Marlene?" I offered. "There's plenty of room."

Marlene nodded. "I don't think I could drive," she said through her tears.

When Ettie was leaving later that night, she apologized again to Marlene.

Marlene said she didn't hold anything against her or the police. She was just shocked that her husband could hurt someone.

I walked Ettie and Elsa-May to the front door.

"I feel bad for ruining the night, Molly."

"I've got quite a bit of food left over. At least I won't have to cook for a week." I tried to cover my annoyance with humor. I didn't blame Ettie and I was glad the killer was found, but I was disappointed that my first time entertaining with Jazeel had ended so uncomfortably.

"I'll walk with you to the phone," Jazeel said to the elderly sisters.

"It's not necessary, it's not far."

"I'd feel better if I wait with you for the taxi."

Ettie nodded. "We'd appreciate that."

Three people left the house, and now I was left alone with the woman who'd just found out that her husband killed her father. I couldn't imagine the things that would be running through her mind.

She was staring at a blank wall. I put my hand on her shoulder and said, "I'll just make up your bed."

"Thank you, Molly," she said in a small voice.

CHAPTER 20

THE NEXT MORNING over the breakfast table, Elsa-May asked, "How are you feeling today, Ettie?"

"Dreadful, just dreadful. If Detective Kelly hadn't asked me to do that I never would've done it. When I told Kelly the knife was missing, he said Max wasn't the sharpest tool in the shed and we might be able to make him confess, but I feel awful the way it happened." Ettie stared into her hot tea.

"And so you should."

Ettie whipped her head up. "What do you mean?"

"It was Molly's night. It was her big dinner, and you ruined it."

Ettie slumped further down on the kitchen chair dropping her shoulders. "At least we know who killed Uncle Alfie now."

"We do."

"Do you think we should visit Molly and apologize again?"

"We?"

"Well, just me if you won't come with me."

"You did enough apologizing last night. I don't think that'll help anything. Just leave her be for a few days."

Ettie nodded. "Something's been nagging at me. Max didn't exactly confess."

"Ettie, the man said he'd been wearing gloves when you talked about the knife, what more of a confession do you need?"

The thing that's running through my mind is his last words as he ran out of the house. *I didn't do it.*"

"*Jah,* and if I was facing what he's facing now I'd probably deny it too, even if I'd done it."

Ettie pulled her mouth to one side.

"What now?" Elsa-May asked.

"Something's been bothering me about the neighbor."

"His messy house? His patchy uneven facial hair? His full ashtrays lying around his house? The fact that he has no garden in front of the—?"

"If you would be quiet for two seconds, I might be able to think." Ettie pushed her teacup toward Elsa-May. "If you want to be useful, make me another cup, please."

"Okay."

"Shhhh." Ettie drummed her fingertips on her chin

while her sister fixed the tea. She kept thinking and thinking about the neighbor. "That's it. We'll have to visit him again."

"Really? Me too?"

Ettie stared at Elsa-May, who'd just rejoined her at the table. "I'm not going on that long bus ride alone."

"Can I talk now?" Elsa-May asked while passing Ettie a second cup of tea.

"Jah."

"I'll make us some sandwiches for the trip."

Ettie nodded and then took a sip of hot tea. *"Denke."*

WHILE THEY WAITED FOR A TAXI, Ettie had the idea to call the retired Detective Crowley, figuring he might remember Bruno Gillespie.

"Ronald?"

"Is that you, Ettie?"

"Yes, it is I."

"I haven't heard from you in a long time. Is Elsa-May okay? Are you okay?"

"We're fine. She's standing right next to me. What I called about is to ask you if you know a man called Bruno Gillespie."

Crowley chuckled. "Do I know him? I must've arrested him around fifteen times. What's he done now?"

Ettie told him what had happened, with the murder, the semi-confession from Max, the diamond and the fact that Uncle Alfie had reportedly had some damaging information or some kind of evidence that would put Bruno Gillespie in prison for a long time. She ended with, "Bruno had a solid alibi according to Detective Kelly."

"There was a bank robbery that I had been trying to tie him to, but that's going back a good ten years now. I could never pin it on him. Two of his men were shot dead in the bank."

"His men?"

"Men who'd worked for him before. Fewer members in the gang meant fewer people to share in the spoils."

"If Alfie had proof of that, what kind of proof would he have had?"

"It could be anything. It could be plans of the bank, written agreements between the gang members, stuff like that, but the thing is, Ettie, how would Alfie have been in a position to get any of that? If you find that out, that should lead you to what it was that he had."

Ettie was suddenly dug in the ribs by Elsa-May. "Taxi's here."

Ettie gave her sister a quick scowl while rubbing her side. She could've broken one of her ribs, Elsa-May had poked her so hard. "Thank you, Ronald. Our taxi is here and then we have to get a bus for a long journey. We're off to visit Alfie's neighbor, Paul."

"Good luck. And keep out of trouble."

Ettie hung up the receiver.

After a taxi ride, a bus trip and another taxi ride, they finally arrived at Uncle Alfie's next-door neighbor's house in the early afternoon.

They knocked on the door and waited.

"Knock again, Ettie."

Ettie knocked again and, when no one answered, she walked over to a window and looked in. She could see Dave peeping over the kitchen countertop, and he stood up when he saw her. "He's in there," Ettie told her sister.

They listened to Dave unlatch a few locks on the door before he opened it.

"Come in. Sorry about that." He latched the door behind them and then looked up and down the street from the window.

Ettie stared at him. "What are you scared of, Dave?"

"Alfie was murdered and they might come after me."

Elsa-May and Ettie exchanged glances.

"Do you know anything about Max Clark?" Elsa-May asked.

Ettie asked, "Or what about Bruno Gillespie?"

Dave recoiled in horror. "What do *you* know about Gillespie?"

Elsa-May stepped forward. "Why don't you tell us what you know about him, Dave?"

Seeing Dave's hands trembling, Ettie grabbed his

arm and led him to the couch. "Let's sit down and you can tell us all about it."

Dave sat down and folded his arms across his chest. "I'm in danger and so will you be. You shouldn't have come here. He could be watching the place. I could be next."

"Are you scared Gillespie might kill you, too?"

He nodded.

"So you know for a fact Bruno Gillespie killed Alfie?"

He nodded again.

"You saw him?"

"I saw him leaving. I didn't know he'd killed him."

"You need to tell the police."

Dave shook his head. "I'll be next."

"Why do you say that, Dave?" Elsa-May asked.

Dave shook his head and reached for a cigarette. "Mind if I smoke?"

"That's fine," Ettie said even though she did mind. Her clothes stank of smoke after the last time they were at his house. Still, it might calm his nerves and get him to tell them what was going on.

He popped the cigarette into his mouth and lit the end with a lighter. After that, he threw the lighter back on the coffee table and inhaled deeply, held his breath for a moment, and exhaled a cloud of smoke.

"If you're scared of this man, you should definitely go to the police," Elsa-May said. "Do you think he knew you saw him leaving?"

"Dunno."

"Then what?" Ettie asked.

The man took another long drag on his cigarette.

Ettie leaned forward. "Do you know what information Alfie had about Gillespie?"

His eyes fastened onto Ettie. "You know?"

"I think I do."

"You're in danger too."

"That's why you should tell the police and they'll put him away."

"You can't live like this, Dave. Locking your door and being too scared to leave the house," Elsa-May said.

"I dunno."

"How did Alfie know Gillespie?"

"From the bar. There was a group of us that hung out together there. But Alfie and I didn't know Gillespie was a criminal."

"When did you find out?"

He shook his head. "If you don't know, I shouldn't tell you." He turned to Ettie. "Do you really know?"

"I know a bit, and you can tell us the rest."

He puffed on his cigarette and blew the smoke into the air. "It was years ago. Gillespie asked Alfie to drive him and some men somewhere. Alfie was easy-going and did whatever anyone asked. Alfie grew wary when he drove Gillespie and three men down a dark alley. Then they pulled on black ski masks and Gillespie pulled out a gun and ordered Alfie to wait. Alfie told me he was scared stiff, so he waited. Gillespie came back an hour later with a large black bag, and he was by himself."

Ettie recalled the story about the bank job where the men were left dead in the bank. The pieces of the puzzle were fitting together. Alfie had been the reluctant driver of the getaway car.

"When they got back to the bar, Gillespie pulled out a handful of notes from the bag and told Alfie to keep his mouth shut. Alfie gave the money to his wife and told her he'd won a competition and she could do whatever she liked with the money. He said he wanted no part of the money."

The diamond! Ettie thought.

"Then what?" Elsa-May asked.

"I knew something was bothering him and then Emily started talking about winning money and he didn't seem excited about it. One night he was over here and we were both drinking. We often hung out together, watching TV or playing darts. He told me what had happened, and I remembered I was there that night when Gillespie asked him to drive him and some of his friends somewhere."

"Why did he kill him so long after it happened? Why not back then?"

"Yes, he killed his other two friends in the bank," Ettie said.

Dave shrugged and grunted. "He went away soon after for some lesser robberies."

"While he was in jail he probably had time to think about it. Alfie was the only person who could link him to murdering his accomplices and to the bank robbery," Ettie said.

"Yeah, Alfie and whoever Alfie had told about it. I'm worried that Alfie told Gillespie he'd told me."

Ettie patted him on his shoulder. "If that was the case, he'd probably have killed you on the very same night."

"Do you think so?"

"Yes. And just in case I'm wrong, you should really tell the police all you know."

He sniffed, leaned forward and stubbed his cigarette out onto a dirty dinner plate that sat on his coffee table. "I guess I'm damned either way—if I do or if I don't."

Ettie and Elsa-May stayed silent.

"I don't wanna be a snitch."

"Well, you don't want to be dead either, do you?"

"Nah." He sighed. "I'll call the detective. He gave me his card."

Very good, thought Ettie.

He stood and walked over to the kitchen, picked up a card and then grabbed his phone's receiver.

Ettie and Elsa-May waited while he called Detective Kelly. When he was finished he sat back down.

"I told him it was urgent I speak with him and he said he's coming here now."

Ettie stood. "We should leave."

"No. Can't you wait with me until he comes?"

"You want us to?" Elsa-May asked, pulling a face.

Ettie knew Elsa-May wanted to get out of there fast before the detective saw them there. Kelly wouldn't be too happy with them for what he called meddling.

"Yeah."

Dave was fidgeting and so nervous Ettie had to agree to wait. "Okay, we'll stay with you, but as soon as he arrives, he'll want to speak with you in private."

He nodded. "Fair enough."

Ettie recalled Max said he'd worn gloves when handling the knife. "Was Max in the house when Gillespie murdered Alfie?"

"He came soon after and then left in a hurry."

"Didn't you think it strange his son-in-law visited him when he hadn't seen him for years?"

"No. His daughter kept away from him, but Max called in every now and again to check that he was okay. Max told Alfie never to tell his daughter he visited—she's got a temper."

"Tell us how you found Alfie."

"When the housekeeper didn't show with dinner, I went to see if he had any. I was going to order us some pizza. That's when I found him." He shook his head. "I should've known what had happened when I saw Gillespie there. Last thing I heard about him he was in prison."

"Why did you tell us about Joe Mulligan selling the drugs when we came here?"

"That happened. I wasn't making it up."

. . .

When they saw the detective's car pull up outside the house, Ettie asked to borrow the phone. She called for a taxi.

Dave opened the door to greet the detective, and then Ettie and Elsa-May hurried past Kelly with him staring open-mouthed at them.

"Hi, and goodbye, ladies. I'll be in touch," Kelly called after them as they hurried out into the front yard.

They waited for the taxi at the front of the house.

"What do you make of it all, Ettie?"

"I think he's telling the truth."

"What about Max saying he used gloves to hold the murder weapon?" Elsa-May said.

"Yes, that's odd. Perhaps he was covering up and hid the weapon thinking his wife did it?"

"Hmm."

Ettie sniffed her clothes. "I can't wait to get home and out of these clothes."

"Jah, you stink of smoke."

"So do you," Ettie said.

Elsa-May chuckled. "I suppose I do."

CHAPTER 21

I'D JUST FINISHED FEEDING Tom his breakfast when I heard a car. When I looked out the window I saw Ettie and Elsa-May getting out of a taxi.

I turned back to Tom, still eating in the kitchen. "We've got visitors. Be a good boy and stay in here." When I leaned down to touch him, his fur bristled, so I figured I shouldn't touch him when he was eating. Some cats don't like that.

When I opened the door, Ettie and Elsa-May stood there smiling, and Ettie held a tray in her hands.

"We've brought something to say we're sorry," Ettie said.

"Sorry for what?"

"For ruining your night."

"Oh, don't you worry about that. Come on in."

Ettie put a foot in the doorway and looked around. "Where's the cat?"

"Tom's closed in the kitchen. Don't worry, he won't escape."

"*Jah,* that's what I was concerned about," Ettie said as she stepped inside. Elsa-May followed behind her.

When Ettie passed me the tray, I lifted the tea towel and saw chocolate chip cookies—my favorite. *"Wunderbaar!* I love chocolate chip cookies. Sit down and I'll put the kettle on." I whizzed into the kitchen knowing Tom would be okay because the front door was shut. He sauntered out to see our visitors while I filled the teakettle and placed cups on a tray and filled the teapot with tea leaves.

"Have you heard anything from the detective?" I asked them when I joined them in the living room.

"Nothing new. We saw him yesterday."

"And we're hoping for new developments."

"Like what? We already know that Max killed Uncle Alfie."

Ettie and Elsa-May looked at each other.

"What is it?"

Just as Ettie opened her mouth to speak I heard a car. "Who's that?" I stood up and looked out the window to see Detective Kelly getting out. "It's the detective." I opened the door quickly, quite forgetting about Tom.

Tom whizzed between my legs and down the steps

at the front of the house. "Quick, catch him!" I yelled to the detective.

Detective Kelly crouched down and Tom stopped running. Soon Tom was rubbing himself against the detective and letting him stroke his fur.

"He likes you," I said, happy that Tom was calming down.

Kelly scooped him into his arms and carried him inside. Once they were inside, I closed the door and Kelly placed Tom on the floor. When the detective saw Ettie and Elsa-May, he said, "I was hoping you two would be here. I have news."

At that moment, the kettle whistled. "Hold that thought. Hot tea, Detective Kelly?"

He nodded. "Yes, please."

When I sat down with them and everyone had tea, the detective relayed a story about how Uncle Alfie was killed.

"Alfie had unknowingly been the getaway driver for a friend, who paid him money after he'd done it. Alfie gave the money to his wife, telling her he'd won a competition and he wanted her to spend the money on herself. She'd bought a diamond, the one the housekeeper now has. Alfie's son-in-law, Max, secretly used to visit Alfie to make sure he was okay. When he arrived to see Alfie murdered, he was certain his wife had done it so he put gloves on and tried to hide anything that might implicate his wife, and that included hiding the murder weapon."

Ettie interrupted, "Why would he have put gloves on?"

"To hide his prints," Kelly explained.

"And how did Max and Marlene's knife get there?" Elsa-May asked. "Wasn't that the murder weapon?"

"No. Like Max said he had told his wife, the knife was in his garage waiting for him to get around to sharpening it. He took the bloody knife he found in Alfie's house and threw it in a dumpster, and he was wearing gloves when he did that."

"Oh, dear. I feel bad for what I said to him the other night," Ettie said. "He must've got confused and ran out when he thought what he said sounded like he'd murdered Alfie."

"I'm the one to blame," Detective Kelly said. "I thought he was guilty and I put you up to it."

Ettie sighed. "I was wrong when I told you about the knife, though."

"So Max is innocent?" I asked.

"He tampered with evidence, but once we told him we had the real killer, Bruno Gillespie, he gave us a full statement, and we released him."

"Have you arrested Bruno Gillespie?" Ettie asked.

"Yes. Thanks to Dave, the neighbor."

Ettie tapped a thin bony finger on her chin. "Jazeel told us his uncle told him he was hiding evidence about Gillespie."

"Things get mixed up slightly when they're passed

on from one person to another. The evidence was in Alfred's head, he could have testified against him. Gillespie admitted to doing a little looking around for the cash he'd given Alfred all those years ago, thinking he might still have it hidden somewhere in the house."

Elsa-May asked, "What about Gillespie's rock solid alibi?"

"We checked a little further into that. He was with a parole officer most of the day. When we questioned the parole officer again, he admitted to blacking out. Gillespie had slipped him something, drugged his coffee, and the officer thought his job was on the line if he told us. He only admitted it when he knew we had Gillespie's confession."

"So all's well that ends well?" I said to the detective, hoping that everything was solved.

"I think we can safely say that."

And all was well with me. I had my Tom and God had given me another chance with Jazeel. We were marrying in two months.

Tom jumped onto the couch next to the detective.

"I've rarely seen him get on the couch before. He almost always hides under it," I said.

"He's such a lovely cat," Kelly said, smoothing down his fur. "Look at those eyes."

Tom stared adoringly at Kelly and then leaned against him, purring all the while.

I noticed Ettie and Elsa-May smiling at each other. I

knew my new elderly friends were wishing they had a lovely cat like Tom rather than their fluffy, white yapping dog?

Thank you for reading 'The Amish Cat Caper.'

THE NEXT BOOK IN THE SERIES

Book 12 Lost

Stumbling onto secrets or skeletons? When Ettie's dog unearths human bones in a field, she unexpectedly finds herself implicated in a cold case murder mystery. In her quest to clear her name, Ettie crosses paths with an Amish woman, Gertie, who spins a chilling yarn of two 'accidental' deaths.

Initially, Ettie dismisses these tales as fanciful fictions until Gertie herself vanishes. Was Gertie weaving tall tales or narrating deadly truths? Can Ettie 'dig up' her memory of Gertie's tales to follow the breadcrumb trail?

Or will Gertie end up another 'unfortunate accident' on the record?

Join Ettie on a twisty journey into the bone-chilling

tales of the Amish countryside, where truth is stranger than fiction, and 'accidents' may not be accidents at all.

ABOUT SAMANTHA PRICE

Samantha Price is a USA Today bestselling and Kindle All Stars author of Amish romance books and cozy mysteries. She was raised Brethren and has a deep affinity for the Amish way of life, which she has explored extensively with over a decade of research.

She is mother to two pampered rescue cats, and a very spoiled staffy with separation issues.

www.SamanthaPriceAuthor.com

Click here to view (or download) a series reading order of all Samantha Price's books.

Watch Samantha's YouTube channel and listen to some of her Audiobooks for free. When you get there, be sure to SUBSCRIBE and click the notifications bell so you don't miss any future audiobooks.

ETTIE SMITH AMISH MYSTERIES

Book 1 Secrets Come Home
Book 2 Amish Murder
Book 3 Murder in the Amish Bakery
Book 4 Amish Murder Too Close
Book 5 Amish Quilt Shop Mystery
Book 6 Amish Baby Mystery
Book 7 Betrayed
Book 8 Amish False Witness
Book 9 Amish Barn Murders
Book 10 Amish Christmas Mystery
Book 11 The Amish Cat Caper
Book 12 Lost: Amish Mystery
Book 13 Amish Cover-Up
Book 14 The Last Word
Book 15 Old Promises
Book 16 Amish Mystery at Rose Cottage
Book 17 Plain Secrets

ETTIE SMITH AMISH MYSTERIES

Book 18 Fear Thy Neighbor
Book 19 Amish Winter Murder Mystery
Book 20 Amish Scarecrow Murders
Book 21 Threadly Secret
Book 22 Sugar and Spite
Book 23 A Puzzling Amish Murder
Book 24 Amish Dead and Breakfast
Book 25 Amish Mishaps and Murder
Book 26 A Deadly Amish Betrayal
Book 27 Amish Buggy Murder

ALL SAMANTHA PRICE BOOK SERIES

Amish Maids Trilogy

Amish Love Blooms

Amish Misfits

The Amish Bonnet Sisters

Amish Women of Pleasant Valley

Ettie Smith Amish Mysteries

Amish Secret Widows' Society

Expectant Amish Widows

Seven Amish Bachelors

ALL SAMANTHA PRICE BOOK SERIES

Amish Foster Girls

Amish Brides

Amish Romance Secrets

Amish Christmas Books

Amish Wedding Season

Printed in Great Britain
by Amazon